PENGUIN
STAMFORD

Thammika Songkaeo is a trained writer, and film producer of Thai origin, whose lived experiences in India, Uganda, Rwanda, the United States, and Singapore have informed the making of *Stamford Hospital*, her debut novel following a nomination to the Bread Loaf Environmental Writers Conference, which she attended on a Katharine Bakeless Nason Scholarship, a fellowship to the Comparative Literature PhD programme of the University of Texas at Austin, and a grant from the Smithsonian Freer | Sackler Galleries.

She earned the highest honours for her study of French Literature at Williams College and an MFA in Creative Nonfiction from the Vermont College of Fine Arts before becoming a Storytelling grantee of the National Geographic Society in 2022 and continuing a transnational gaze on stories of the relationship between womanhood and society. Her writing, including a feature of monologues, has appeared in *Ninth Letter* and in *World Literature Today* online, and for the Singapore National Library Board.

When not writing, she can be found working on social and environmental issues through her company, Two Glasses LLP, designing experiences that transform how people think and feel about their identity and planetary mayhem.

ADVANCE PRAISE FOR *STAMFORD HOSPITAL*

'*Stamford Hospital* is a poignant exploration of the silent struggles of a trailing spouse, navigating marriage, motherhood, and identity in a foreign land. A vivid portrait of a woman's longing, loss, and resilience, told with unflinching honesty and emotional depth.'

—Margaret Thomas, founding member of The Association of Women for Action and Research (AWARE)

'*Stamford Hospital* offers a piercing look at the brutal realities faced by women in Singapore, exposing the deep sacrifices and stark power imbalances they endure, especially as trailing spouses. A compelling and challenging read.'

—Corinna Lim, executive director, The Association of Women for Action and Research (AWARE)

'A compelling exploration of the darker tolls that come with motherhood. *Stamford Hospital* unflinchingly confronts a thorny disposition: how to stay sane when everything one could possibly want in life still isn't enough?'

—Parisa Pichitmarn, *South China Morning Post* contributor, freelance journalist, former editor at *Muse*

'A searing and intimate snapshot of the dislocations of motherhood and marriage, interleaved with the dislocations of language, class, and identity that emerge from a truly "culturally amphibious" life in Thailand, America, and Singapore. Tense and engaging, Songkaeo's story stayed with me long after the novel concluded.'

—Roanne Kantor, assistant professor of English, Stanford University

Stamford Hospital

Thammika Songkaeo

PENGUIN BOOKS
An imprint of Penguin Random House

PENGUIN BOOKS

Penguin Books is an imprint of the Penguin Random House group of
companies whose addresses can be found at global.penguinrandomhouse.com

Published by Penguin Random House SEA Pte Ltd
40 Penjuru Lane, #03-12, Block 2
Singapore 609216

First published in Penguin Books by Penguin Random House SEA 2025

Copyright © Thammika Songkaeo 2025

All rights reserved

10 9 8 7 6 5 4 3 2 1

This is a work of fiction. Names, characters, places and incidents
are either the product of the author's imagination or are used fictitiously,
and any resemblance to any actual person, living or dead, events or
locales is entirely coincidental.

Please note that no part of this book may be used or reproduced in any manner
for the purpose of training artificial intelligence technologies or systems.

ISBN 9789815233056

Typeset in Garamond by MAP Systems, Bengaluru, India

This book is sold subject to the condition that it shall not, by way of trade
or otherwise, be lent, resold, hired out, or otherwise circulated without the
publisher's prior consent in any form of binding or cover other than that in
which it is published and without a similar condition including this condition
being imposed on the subsequent purchaser.

www.penguin.sg

CHAPTER 1

The night was dark enough to feel like a cover. It cornered them in their separate shells—three of them in the bedroom, usually three different dreams, each with its own preoccupations, but tonight Tarisa laid awake. They slept in an unusual arrangement for a family that had ample space. Mia always slept with Tarisa and Chris in the master, tucked into a mattress beside their queen bed. Trying to put her in her own room hadn't worked—it had only led to her wailing, waking them up, or standing hauntingly by their bedside before tugging their body parts out to get them to rise and follow her.

The sexlessness of their marriage, which had led to their doing nothing but sleep at night, had helped Tarisa and Chris to decide that it would be fine to add Mia to the master. Her existence, for once, would make no difference.

Tarisa slipped off the bed, swinging her hair to the left. The black, wavy strands draped over her cheek and hung heavy. She walked with her neck and torso bent, following their weight. *I'd tell a stranger that I'm lopsided because my heart is heavy*, she joked to herself.

She had been lying awake for an hour, despite preferring to be asleep. For her, the perfect slumber crept into one's legs and arms as a feeling of levitation, then oozed into the head to make it turn into steam. Skin-to-skin was how she best found her relaxation, but tonight, as usual, her husband had left her contours open and cold. He was holding her for the first few minutes after they had turned the lights off. Then, at some point, he had also drifted off and turned his back to her. She did not turn around to spoon him. Already a light sleeper, he would not appreciate being roused.

She opened the door to the guestroom, where the windows showered her with the view of the dark sky and brightly lit ships. The vast water wasn't the ocean, but the Singapore Strait, dotted with cargo ships—cruising, free. Once docked in the morning, they would look imprisoned, even if the sky promised infinity.

She sat on the bed and for a split-second considered sliding into the balcony and inviting thoughts by the ledge. There were many ways of being alone at night, and the active kind, of entertaining being awake, was not the one that she wanted. She needed to function for others the following day. In the morning, Mia would need to go to school.

She felt, at once, like what was coming up was both her choice and not.

She swept up her legs. Her back seeped into the mattress. Then, she concentrated on the mechanical sounds of the port, before sliding her hand into her husband's boxers, which she was wearing. She wore them because he had many pairs, and she did not see a need to buy her own pyjamas when his extra clothes existed. (She had been told, with regard to this, that she was not the most conventional of people.)

Her mind chose a man from the rolling images in her head. She picked the ex-boyfriend she was most familiar with. He was with her, in imagination, at least twice a week. There was nothing romantic about their imaginary hook-up, no storyline of how they reconnected after they had parted when she was still twenty-one, the age she had met Chris. In her head, she and the ex-boyfriend were already in the act. His eyes were closed as he roamed over her body, his body was heavy, imprinted on hers. She did not mind that they made love without him being able to see her, without him treating her as a person of his affection. What mattered was that she got to be in the act. She wanted, as she had not been for years, to be fucked.

She rubbed herself up and down where it was usually most efficient to. She relied on climaxing by touching herself this way, as she had been doing more often, recently. She wondered if Chris masturbated too.

Then, as she kept repeating the strokes, the wild sensation that she had created reached a dull plateau. She tried to change her rhythm, but the staleness remained.

She paused and restarted, but nothing came to her. She knew, from the way the sensation remained, to stop. She folded her legs together and rolled to one side, letting the failure sink in. She did not know what she had done wrong. At the same time, she considered the fortuity of this development, if she was indeed turning into something closer to her asexual husband. If she was becoming what he was, she might be content, compatible, with him again.

She saw herself from a perspective above the bed. A tiny, young woman, almost tritely foetal, in a time of woe. She could not believe how stereotypical she had become—a housewife, a sad one. There were so many that they were a library genre.

She imagined what was in the master bedroom she had left. Chris was there, turned towards a bay window. If his eyes were open, he would be looking in the same direction as her, seeing a similar view. But he was likely pleasantly circumscribed by his blanket, pulled up to his nose, only his closed eyes to be seen, to be seen not looking at her.

Her tears surfaced, water condensed from a soul. She tried to stay quiet, though she knew his earplugs would keep him from hearing her anyway. That was how much he was closed off in his sleep each night. They lay next to each other on the bed, but it was as if they were on the same ride to different destinations.

Impossible, surely.

It was he who was the (primary) victim of finasteride. She could not let her tears show up too often in front of him. He was the one who was destroyed.

Within a few hours, after sunrise, she would need to pull herself together. He would smile while greeting her, 'Good morning,' and she wouldn't want to ruin his day with what had happened privately to her at night. Then, there was also Mia for whom she would want to have high spirits. 'Good morning, Little Mia,' she would want to say before the girl could ask her what was wrong.

Mia would be able to tell if Tarisa was on the verge of tears, just by her three-year-old's instinct. She would grip onto her mother, probing her mind with a curious tongue until she reached the bones of a response. Tarisa was tired talking to the child, but she knew that, as a mother, she was not to erase her curiosity.

A memory from a year earlier swam into her.

'So, you really don't want to fuck,' she had said to Chris in the bedroom one night, where she was naked on the bed, tears wetting the back of her hands.

'I mean, it's not like that. I want to, but I just can't. I just don't feel it like other men.' He began to apologize, setting his book down on his chest.

He, who had become more fluent in English than in Thai, devouring ideas and norms and making memories in this language just like her, had been reading: a book about partners amid a separation, which she had recommended to him, knowing he'd enjoy the melody of the sentences (even though he might not hear the lyrics; playing jazz on the piano, this inclination towards melody, as opposed to what the singer crooned, often seemed to be his fate).

The protagonist was cold and collected, barely passionate about finding her missing, possibly dead, husband. When Tarisa had been reading it earlier, she had been unable to put the book down. She'd heard the melody and the lyrics—cold Latinate words more suited to an academic study of situations than to the groundwork of love, recorded by a protagonist keeping a discreet eye.

While he was deep into the book, she had had to squeeze her legs together, then turn away to face the wall and the dirty laundry in the hamper to cut herself off from desire, but it wasn't long before she tried to fondle him. He put his book on his tummy, closed his eyes, showing appreciation. She asked—hating to have to—'Can you touch me?' He responded affirmatively, but then he dug her in all sorts of wrong places, the usual. Her body had become a topography that he no longer knew. She asked him to stop, then said, 'Thank you.' She folded away, began to cry. He apologized. She could tell that she had distressed him.

She wanted to hug him and back away from him at the same time. She couldn't control the vacillation—sympathetic one moment, then hateful the next. They both needed sympathy. She loved neither him nor herself enough to ignore either person's predicament.

The next morning, after they woke up, she was unable to look at him when they circulated around the kitchen, preparing Mia's breakfast and lunchbox. He noticed that she was colder.

'What's wrong?' he asked.

'Sex,' she started with just one word, but a whole world was already waiting to burst open. 'Did you know this entire time that you'd one day never be able to? Why didn't you tell me about finasteride before we got married?' She also began to blame herself. When she thought about it, the growing sexlessness had begun showing even before they had married. They had been sleeping together less and less towards the end of their days in America.

'What are you, selfish?' she said, ladling rice into Mia's lunchbox.

His face immediately contorted. She told herself to stay strong and pursue the question she had asked him. She would not let him make her feel like she was picking a fight for nothing. 'Or it's more like you didn't even think about it,' she continued. 'About what this would mean for me.'

'No, T. It's not like that.'

'Then what?'

'I don't know, T!'

'Right. Because you really didn't even think about it.'

'I mean, it's not like that!'

She didn't want to listen any more. 'Because what? Women are supposed to be these virginal people who can't crave anything? It's always supposed to be about you, you, and you? If you want it, you get it. If you don't, well who cares what your wife wants? For the rest of her fucking life.

Is that it? I asked, "Did you know that this would happen before we got married?"'

When she finished her sentence, she realized the irony of the situation. She was yelling at the man who was the victim. She was caning him after his loss.

'I didn't know! I mean, there's no way I could have known!' he said. Mia, whose footsteps they could both hear, ran out of the bedroom. She asked what the noise was about.

'Sorry, sweetheart. We didn't know we ran out of some things we wanted to put in your lunchbox,' Tarisa said.

Mia stood, her belly arching towards her mother, asking what she would get to eat for lunch, in that case.

'Something,' Tarisa said, imagining a bento the kind Japanese mothers are famous for, still feeling the heat from Chris, who hadn't taken his eyes off her. 'Rice. Sausages. Milk. Grapes?' she said, intoning a question at the end.

'I don't like sausages.'

'You do.'

'Not any more.'

Tarisa sighed and reached for a sausage from the fridge, sticking it into the rice, cold.

Mia's hands waved no. 'No, no! I don't like sausages.'

'There's nothing else to eat, Mia.'

'Rice.'

'You need protein.'

'Rice.'

'Is not protein.'

She never resumed the topic again with such fierceness, which she understood did nothing but distress Chris. After all, it might be true that he could not have fathomed the future of his impotence. Yet again, what she had heard underneath his answer was also that he did not care to even consider how her life would have turned out if he had.

In the morning, she autopiloted into the self that she had been carrying.

She dropped Mia off at school on a taxi, then headed for the train home alone. There was no need to pay for a taxi in her solitude; her solo liberty typically made train-taking not a burden. She even felt more comfortable standing in a packed carriage than sitting spaciously in a taxi with a child. The journey during the morning rush hour was usually bland in the pond of phone-scrolling people. The blandness was self-perpetuating—people at the train station looked at their phones because their surroundings bored them, the environment was made boring by people looking at their phones. When she could, Tarisa tried to look at other people's screens to find out what captivated them. She did not use her phone in the same way. She had figured out, since she had quit her job a year and a half ago, that technology didn't help much with isolation.

Tarisa kept a look out for anything that might be residually inspiring. Observations were all she had to make each day unique. She suddenly became overwhelmed as soon as she stepped onto the platform to wait for the train. A 'helper', a woman imported from a poor Southeast Asian country to serve as a maid, was berating a toddler who was trying to hold onto her as if she was the last morsel of food he would ever get to eat.

'Stop it! If you do that again, I will—' the helper said, raising her voice. She stopped before finishing her sentence, surrendering to a wordless violence. She was speaking in an English that reminded Tarisa of the bursts of popcorn. Her eyes also popped out to swallow the boy whole.

The boy, who looked about Mia's age, was gripping onto the fabric of her clothes and pressing his cheek onto the hem of her jean shorts. She yanked him away by gripping the back collar of his preschool uniform. 'Stop it! Stop it! You are a bad, bad boy!' Her voice megaphoned frustration and hatred.

In Myanmar, Tarisa guessed from the Thanaka powder on her face, *she might not be so repressed and eruptive. I can understand the stress of being with a child the whole time. She's come to Singapore to be paid in Singapore dollars, and now she is probably overworked, barely sleeping, and scapegoated for all miseries.*

Tarisa recalled a recent piece of news—a couple deducted a helper's salary because she cut tofu 'wrongly,' as they say here. They bit, scratched, slapped, and scalded her. She scaled down fifteen floors of balconies to save her life.

'Auntie! Auntie!' the boy pleaded, calling her in this term that in the Western world only indicates someone in the family, but is so prevalent here, and incongruous with the sentiments at hand.

In her large, round eyes, Tarisa could see messages rolling through—*I hate you. I hate this. I want to be away, in my own life. Keep your distance.* She also remembered what eyes did—they reflected. She hoped the message wasn't actually her own, towards the life that she knew. She saw herself in every woman frustrated at a child. She wished she didn't, so that instead of seeing herself, she could see where she stood: above standard, standard, or below standard, as a child-rearing woman.

As the train came rolling in, nobody on the platform said anything, including Tarisa, who, on one hand, didn't think the boy should have to go undergo this treatment, but on the other hand, thought that this was a scenario his parents must have considered. No one should romanticize how hired help would treat their child.

She wondered what kind of arrangement was set up for this helper, how the woman slept, ate, and acted when the parents were around. *Probably the stiff silence*. She had seen plenty of women who sat at the sharp edges of dining tables at food courts or restaurants, gazing down, clutching stuffed bags, making sure that they wouldn't fall from the seats. It was their job to haul and protect the family's belongings so that any object summoned by the parents could suddenly materialize. Helpers were supposed to be the genies that made the parents' wishes come true.

'Why don't you just get a helper? It really makes a difference,' acquaintances liked to suggest. Their helpers all looked miserable when they weren't around, but these acquaintances didn't know, or they didn't care. Everyone she had talked to said that their helper was 'great', but that couldn't be so from what Tarisa had seen.

They never saw what happened when their children were alone with the helper. Tarisa sometimes did. Once, she said to another mother at school without thinking, 'Oh, it was so nice to see Giana with your helper yesterday, Camilla. They were holding hands. It was a lovely sight, you know, because usually your helper is just walking in front—'

'She's usually walking *in front*?' Camilla interrupted.

'Yes, usually, she's walking in front, but—'

'You mean on the street?'

'Well, I mean the sidewalk—'

'She wasn't holding Giana's hand?'

'No, not usually, but yesterday—'

Tarisa watched as, behind Camilla's look of surprise, the image of her helper's affectionate relationship with her child melted away. Had she never expected the woman—the stranger introduced to their home—to be anything less than genuinely, perennially attentive? *Even mothers break.*

'My helper is the best,' she had heard another woman say to a new mother, a recent addition from Europe. Tarisa wanted to tell her that when she wasn't there, the helper would yank her child's arm and toss her into the taxi, once even forgetting to close the door. The European, still amazed to be able to afford live-in help here, was enthused by the prospect of having time to herself, with just a little help from a Southeast Asian woman.

What did these mothers know? The ones who give their children to someone else.

Tarisa kept her eye on the helper and this stranger's child as she boarded the train at nine o'clock. The boy—now limp—was not holding onto the pole, his helper was not holding onto him, and none of the adults were giving up their seats. Everybody looked at only their phones. Tarisa gripped onto the handrail and kept her eyes on his life.

Four years ago, at the news of her pregnancy, Tarisa and Chris briefly discussed getting a helper. 'I would want the woman to have her own room. A proper room, not the storage room, so that she can be happy,' she had said.

'Most people put their helpers in the storage room,' he replied, not looking at her, instead lifting dirt off his Steinway & Sons grand piano with a soft cloth.

'But we won't.'

'We *can*.'

She held back her words. At times, he could be uninterested in understanding other people's ideals. He had grown up privileged, with his own maids in a separate quarter in his childhood home in Bangkok. He had never looked at helpers as equal humans.

'Can we agree to disagree?' he said.

She had heard this question many times and knew that there was no hope talking to him when he said this. 'Obviously, yes. That's always technically a possibility, but you do realize that a woman living in a storage room isn't a happy woman, and you can't have an unhappy woman being a nanny to our child. For her to have her own space, we'd need a different place.'

'No, you're right, but I don't want to move.' He looked at the floor, sighed, and listed the reasons—this apartment was across the street from his office; it was also modern, new, and breezy. He also tried, knowing that she had a penchant for frugality, 'Even if we moved in nine months, we would still break the lease and have to pay the penalty.'

'*Can't* we break the lease? You're choosing between breeze and our baby's well-being.'

'It's a lot of money, Tarisa. Money isn't just something you throw here and there according to what you want, now, then now, then now, then now.'

'I'm not asking for now, then now, then now, then now. It's our child, Chris. The lease can be broken. A maid in a storage room will mean hell.'

'For whom?'

'The maid and therefore the baby. Come on, that was obvious.'

He looked at her in disbelief, this potential of rift between them unexpected. 'I don't know how we're gonna put her in a bedroom.'

She looked at him, the image of him captured by her mind's eye thinning out. Instead, she saw the room they were standing in, precisely the room that Tarisa thought could be the helper's. He sat down on the piano stool and began to play a jazz song, a classic that she couldn't identify.

At half past nine now, she was standing in a grocery store. Her phone rang. It was the school.

'Mia's mommy?' the voice broke in.

'Yes, that's me.' She wished she had been addressed by her name, an old, important artefact that had seemed to go missing when she became 'Mia's mother'.

'Mia's coughing. You need to come and pick her up.'

A part of Tarisa had seen this call coming. Early signs of a cold had swept through breakfast. Nevertheless, she let out a sigh, not minding that the staff on the line could hear. (Coming off as the perfect mother was not a part of her plans. She was the youngest mother at the school, a superlative that she assumed allowed room for creating mistakes.)

In the aisle, bright bags of popcorn competed for her attention while she continued to grip onto her phone. She chose the brand with the least artificial ingredients, which, in some books, would have made her a decent mother, so she silently congratulated herself. Pulling it off the shelf, she could not stop thinking that it was she, and not Chris, who was getting the call. She wished *he* would be the one to suddenly need to drop what he was doing right now. She wished *he* would do the journeys to and from school. She wished *he* would have to be flexible when their child was sick.

She had always wondered whether having an office to go to kept Chris from wanting to distance himself from Mia, the way that she often did. When she was still a working mother, she had wanted to see Mia at the end of the day. She and Chris split childcare equally in terms of hours, as she tallied, but he had always been able to hold onto a job while she would eventually—and she couldn't stop wondering if the fault was hers—be left with none.

As upset as Tarisa was thinking about the school's call, as she was upset every time that she saw in the emergency contact list that those listed were always the mothers, she knew that it was they—she and Chris, like the other parent couples—who had decided to write down the mother's name, though they both were equally tied up at work back then.

Between them, there had been an incident before Mia's conception that had led her to know that he had expected her to be the more flexible one. She called what had happened 'that October', and soon, she would be thinking about it again.

She began towards a taxi to pick Mia up now. She wished to be a responsible parent who went to pick up a sick child fast, which meant not crawling to school on a train, then a little more on foot. There was no public transport near the school in a rich neighbourhood, where most people got around in thick, long sedans. She had not bought one for herself.

The driver thought he could know more about her.

'Where are you from?' he said.

'Thailand.' Her body sunk a fraction of an inch, trying to retreat from the conversation, but the seat kept her from escaping farther away.

'Don't look Thai. Also never see Thai people with good English. Why you speak good English?'

She readied a form of imperfect English, hoping it would stave off inquiries about her household income, which drivers here were quick to ask about when noticing a certain combination of English and race. 'Lived in America.' She dreaded the direction the conversation threatened to go.

'And why no look Thai?'

'Half. Mom Teochew.' Every time, summoning her mother's roots made her think about her mother's stories of childhood, how she had to sell soda on the streets to help her parents make a living in Thailand's countryside after they had sailed away from a Chinese one. Leela was proud of Tarisa for going to America for university on a scholarship, failing to consider that Tarisa had ended up an anonymous full-time mother like herself.

'Can speak Teochew? I also Teochew.' He continued in speech presumably that.

'Don't understand. Mom born in Thailand. Mom speak Thai.'

'America since young, ah?'

'Yeah, since young.' It didn't matter that her English would flow more like a river if this had been true. If his lie detector would go off and a great abyss would emerge between them, he could do the work—to her amusement—of further pursuing the truth eagerly. She looked out of his scratched window at the dreamy, large homes of politicians and billionaires. The thick, white fluffy dogs that the uniformed maids were walking looked richer than the women tugging their leash.

The truth, which she didn't give to him, was chopped up kaleidoscopically. A piece of herself had grown in

India, another in Rwanda, another in the United States, and many more. Her father, a diplomat for Thailand, brought them abroad, feeding the family with dignity and culture more than his pay. Financial aid had allowed her to study at Middlebury, Berkeley, and Harvard, the last at which, had things gone her way, 'that October' would never have happened. She would be in a doctoral cap and gown around now.

As the taxi approached the country club housing Mia's school, she rolled her window down and nodded to the guard, putting on a sweet, playful face, important for her to still know she could have. With the push of a button, he let her through. This man, whom she had never seen speaking to the European members of the club, occasionally made conversation with her. Once, he licked his lips as she walked by, rocking her confidence with his appetite. Maybe she was sleezy, sordid, unvaluable, after all.

'Uncle, *zhe bien, xie xie.*' She let the taxi know where to stop. She paid him thirteen dollars and forty cents, exactly as the meter asked. Despite a tipless culture, some drivers pretended there was no situation for change. She wanted to prevent feeling cheated.

'*Hua yu ye ke yi,* ah?' He was surprised to find out she could speak Mandarin. 'Means you live in Singapore long time already, ah?'

'*Yi dian dian.* Five years. Thank you.' She explained that she spoke only a little Mandarin. She closed the car door softly, just firm enough to be sure the door had latched. Closing a door with a bang seemed to say one couldn't care less about what happened to someone else's property.

Her mother had taught her that the way you close a door expresses who you are.

There were no long lines or red tape for her to enter the school. Looking beyond, she could see club members relaxing in groups under a tiki hut. They were mostly European and white. A few Asian members, mostly wives of the men, added people who looked closer to her in the mix. Most of them, still, had fairer skin. Tarisa's was a mix of Leela's warm beige and her father's southern-Thai chestnut. Those who tried to understand her by her skin tone, where their minds grouped her in with 'a certain group of Thai women', sometimes voiced their assumptions through their questions—*'You speak very good English. Is your husband white?'*

It was frustratingly unpredictable, the question of from whom or when the assumptions would come. If she was not a *farang*-hunting Thai woman, then she might be something else, which was still not her.

Once, when Tarisa had decided to wear only a T-shirt and jean shorts, dressing as the European mothers did, a white teacher said, 'Thank you. Good service,' as she held the door. Tarisa fought back that evening in a prideful email to the principal, describing what had happened in consciously eloquent English, the way she had wanted to write a dissertation. She received an apology, and from then on, always looked at the teacher in question with what she thought was superior forgiveness.

Today, Tarisa was in a linen dress and diamond earrings. She alternated between natural fibres and jean shorts, the latter which she wore on purpose to test whether their prejudice had waned. As she walked, she watched a family of monkeys sitting on top of a steel gate. The adult monkey looked back at her while the offspring switched positions, running amok with their siblings. People—mostly strangers who gave their unsolicited opinion—expected her to have a family like this, with more than one child. 'More natural,' they said.

She walked towards the school office with the bag of popcorn hanging in her hands. She saw and heard the older children out in recess laughing, boys passing balls while girls chattered hand in hand. *Gendered.* 'She's cannot find she's snack,' a girl she knew, raised multilingual like many kids at school, said. Mia, too, used to speak like this. But now, her English was outgrowing her Thai.

Mia will probably ask for popcorn before saying, 'Hello, Mommy.'

Tarisa was tired just thinking that she would have to remind the girl to have manners. They might even have a small argument about it. Tarisa wished she had a place to hide the popcorn, that she had not refused the paper bag at the store. She wanted Mia to eat, but first, to be polite. Her politeness would help Tarisa feel that she, herself, was not taken for granted.

There she was. Mia was looking at her through the glass door. No sign of pleasure decorated her face. Her round head sat delicately on her small pod of a body. Her round eyes twinkled only faintly, barely lighting her up.

Put on a happy face. It helps to set the mood you prefer.

Tarisa swung open the door, pushing instead of pulling, directing her energy in towards Mia. The little girl said nothing. She only blinked, giving Tarisa the idea that their afternoon together might house long naps and torpor.

'I heard someone's coughing!' Tarisa said in a singsong voice, testing Mia one more time. She realized that she wanted Mia to continue her calmness, and that she had interpreted that calmness as Mia barely existing. Normally a chatty and exhausting child, Mia could create sentences and conversations that many children her age could not—delightful to witness but exhausting to interact with.

At her two-year-old health check a year ago, the doctor had asked how many words Mia could speak in a phrase. 'Two or three?' he offered. Tarisa became confused. 'Twelve,' she said. 'In a sentence.' She realized only then that she might have a gifted child.

Mia usually made her animated mind so transparent. Her quietness now made Tarisa flounder. She wanted to know if Mia was all right, if she was thinking and activated inside, but she feared opening an endless conversation if she asked. She turned away to the staff who had been working at her desk next to Mia and thanked her.

'No problem at all. She was very easy,' the woman said.

Very easy. Tarisa felt judged. *You don't know what she can be like.* She knew that the woman was not wrong, that during the time in which she sat on that couch, Mia had not caused trouble. Yet, she could not help but think that Mia was playing angelic for everyone but her. It was a thought that she immediately recognized as unreasonable. Certainly, Mia was not dividing up the world into her mother whom she would damage and others whom she would spare. And yet, Tarisa knew that her fatigue—and those memories of Mia being much less than pleasant, crying diabolically or wanting constant entertainment—must have come from real events. Tarisa wanted the world to see what made up her exhaustion, which rested at the lobby of her disposition, available for collision and eruption anytime. The morsels of her that felt provoked, tiptoeing on her sanity's limits, had difficulty hearing Mia described as 'very easy', a term that seemed to question her memory and the deep chambers of rancour to which it led.

'Are you hungry, sweetheart? I have popcorn,' Tarisa said, moving forward with a bitter feeling. She squatted on the floor next to Mia and shook the bag.

'Now?'

'No, later. When we're home, so that you can have a drink with it. Otherwise, you might cough even more.'

'Can I have it now?'

'Not yet, sweetie. I just explained why.'

'I like popcorn.'

'I know. Let me call a car.'

She could have asked the taxi driver who had brought her here to wait, but he had been too chatty, unusable for her need to save energy to expend on Mia in the whole afternoon that lay ahead. (Even if Chris' salary could afford a car in this country where car ownership was notoriously expensive, Tarisa preferred public transport, shared rides, or taxis. For her, economizing was a habit from childhood. For Chris, frugality was an amusing muscle to exercise. His frugality had come, at first, out of trying to placate Tarisa and her ways. Then, as he discovered through practice that public transport was efficient in Singapore, he never considered getting a car again.) A new taxi arrived five minutes later, which should have pleased a passenger, but Tarisa found this unfavourable, a hindrance to her desire to stand in place, where she was receiving an expansive, returned quietness from her child. Who knows how time together at home would unfold?

Her back bent in the taxi's doorway as she secured Mia into her portable car seat, Tarisa felt the bolded sunlight on her neck. She continued to tug, snap, and tighten the harnesses and Velcro of the car seat, doing so quickly to escape the heat, constantly surprised by how much Mia trusted her to carry out these actions, while her little body was knocked around.

'Say, "Hello Uncle", please, Mia,' Tarisa said, checking for the final bits of security.

Mia said nothing.

'You still have to be polite even if you're sick, sweetheart.'

'Hello.'

'Tired?'

'Yeah.'

'You can get plenty of rest when you get home, okay?'

'I don't want to rest. I want to play. Can we play Barbie together?'

Shit. Barbies. Talking. Barbies.

'Let me get in the car first, then we'll talk,' Tarisa said to buy time, even if it was a few seconds.

She took her seat, saw Mia had put her thumb in her mouth, and pulled it out.

'No. There's germs on your thumb. No.'

Mia pulled her thumb back in again.

'No! No means no! You'll only get sicker and sicker if you do that, and God knows what that might involve.' When she finished her sentence, she gazed at Mia for a second too long, wondering what the trajectory of her sickness was currently destined to be. Mia looked right back at her, the prolonged way only a child's guiltless curiosity knew how to. At this reciprocation, which felt uncomfortable, Tarisa knew that she had made herself an interesting mould of emotions for Mia to observe, and now, she was afraid that the child would inquire about what she was seeing. She broke their stare and drove her gaze forward, an effort to save herself from potentially being questioned.

The taxi climbed slowly out of the driveway, exhaling a brake when a little monkey ran across alone. It was scrambling, a little lost, like it was finding the others. Strangers had told her that that was what she was making of Mia by having an only child.

'About the Barbies,' Tarisa returned to the old subject, thinking it would be smarter to talk about dolls, a conversation that could end more quickly than one about what the previous, reciprocated gazing meant, 'I need to make you lunch.'

'It's okay. I'm not hungry,' Mia said.

'But it will be time to eat lunch,' Tarisa said, continuing, even knowing that lunch shouldn't be for another hour and a half. The priority right now was to draw Mia's interest away from the potential of talking about what had seemed to Tarisa a theatre of gaze.

'But can we play Barbie first?'

Good, good, good. Let's talk about Barbies, much easier than deconstructing my feelings. We don't need to talk about my anxiety when I think about a whole afternoon with you.

'No. First, I'll make you lunch,' she said, waving goodbye to the guard.

In the empty streets now, she leaned her head onto the headrest, moving in for a calming posture. She imagined draining her worries to the back of her head. The bump of her bun stopped her from being able to move far. She untied it, rolling her hair tie onto her wrist, where it encircled her loosely, her thin frame not allowing for a more possessive latch. Nothing more to do now, the anxiety about having to play with Barbies returned. She had been wanting to throw away those cumbersome, empty dolls. She wished Leela had never bought them. The purposes of pretend play were clear—why she was glad that Mia was already in a school—but she could not convince herself to power up and start chatting away as if it—essentially ventriloquizing—excited her. If the record had been that what she felt she could offer made do, then she might have felt a little more eager, thinking that she had found an activity that would grease the passage of time, but since the record had been that no words of hers were ever good enough, never a match for what Mia thought her Barbie should say, Tarisa could not stop thinking about Barbies as an exercise of snowballing trials and errors, herself crushed underneath Mia's uncharted, possibly limitless, standards.

'What do you want to do today?' Mia would say.

'Sit down and eat,' I would reply.

'No, no, say, "Go on an airplane".'

'Go on an airplane.'

'Go on an airplane.'

'No, not like that! Say it and get up and take Barbie around the house! Like on a real airplane!'

I might get up. My feet might drag on the floor. I'll try to move as slowly as I can. The short distance I cover can take up a wild amount of time. Or so I'll think before she notices. And shouts, 'Faster! Faster, Mommy, faster!'

I will groan about it. I will tell her that it's not fair, that I'm tired.

Their condo wasn't small, large enough to temporarily hide a withdrawn mother. Tarisa knew what she would do if she took Barbie up and away into a different room—ask this part of the home for shelter. She would see a bed or a couch, plop down on it, and close her eyes, hope that in parallel to the invisibility she was producing for herself, her child in another room had also forgotten about her. Silences of two separate epicentres would ripple through the home, creating concentric shells over herself and Mia, which kept them in the preferred solitude.

But because it felt cruel to be declining Mia's requests so often, Tarisa often yielded, imposing time limits—'fifteen minutes,' 'until the long hand of the clock strikes six,' and so on. To her surprise, time passed faster if she didn't look at the watch always on her wrist.

A few times, Tarisa would wonder if her lethargy was from not eating enough. She would try to snack before or during their time together, on grapes, bananas, crackers—anything that didn't need much effort. She liked things that were easy to pop into her mouth, avoiding more work for herself. Still, those snacks never helped. A health check showed that she also was not anaemic. 'Just really unenthusiastic about playing with my child?' she once asked a doctor, who turned to her despairingly from his screen and said, 'Most likely, yes.'

The last time she had played Barbies, when she had already given up on the idea of trying to enjoy it, she told Mia that her Barbie was 'there, but just thinking quietly'. One minute later, when her Barbie still hadn't budged, Mia shook her mother's doll, then her wrist and her arms. 'Play, Mommy, play!' the girl cried and cried. Tarisa let out a short scream, one antithetical to the calm that she wanted to have. She hit the soft, leather couch, which bounced back as if it understood that it had evolved from loveseat to sandbag. She stood up and stormed into the bedroom, wanting to slam it shut, which she didn't do as she considered that Mia might try to enter the room right when the door would swing; then, the girl would suffer a blow to her entire, three-foot-long body and need to be taken to the hospital, which was not only pitiable, but also practically more work for Tarisa herself. Mia followed her, quickly and closely, gliding easily into the bedroom like Tarisa's own shadow. Tarisa tried to regulate her breath, controlling her mind and whatever might come out of her wild, wet mouth again.

'I like your hair. It's like Barbie's,' Mia said now, in the taxi.

'Yes, Mia; it's wavy like Barbie's, but it's not blonde like Barbie's.'

'I like it.'

'Thanks.'

'I want it.'

'Maybe one day you'll have it. Mine used to be straight like yours when I was a kid.'

'Then what?'

'Then it became wavy.'

'So, when I grow up, I be like you?'

'Guess so. You want to?'

'Yeah. Can I work out with you, Mommy?'

Tarisa looked at her. 'Aren't you sick?'

'No, not really.'

'That was rhetorical. Mia, you're sick.'

'What's ruhdawdial?'

'Rhetorical.'

'Yeah. What's that?'

'It's a question for which I already knew the answer. Its purpose was just to make you think.'

'Then why is it a question?'

Tarisa looked out at the trees and gated homes. Instead of answering Mia right away, she thought about how she had never wanted to live in one of these. They would be too much work. A landed home was a status symbol, but Tarisa couldn't care less about showing people how much she—she corrected herself—*Chris* made, working in an international organization much like the International Monetary Fund, where he had been in Washington, DC, before he suddenly decided to settle here, beginning the rift between them.

She looked at the estimated time of arrival on the driver's GPS, even if she knew the ride would roughly be another twenty minutes. She wanted to know exactly what time she would be home alone with Mia. She spoke into the window, remembering to answer Mia's question. She saw her own reflection, her own lined, dull eyes.

'Because questions make you think.'

'Why questions make you think?'

They were entering a long tunnel, with verdant arches contouring the ceilings.

They don't have this greenery in Bangkok. I'm not here because I want to be, but at least we're not dying in pollution there.

'Mom, I said, "Why questions make you think?"'

'Because you need an answer for them, right? Like, if I shut up right now, would you be okay with it?'

'No!' She roared with laughter, crinkled her nose. Tarisa thought she looked grotesque but also cute.

Hopefully, I don't think she's cute because she looks grotesque. I need to not say 'shut up' again. Last year, she said, 'Fuck!' when she dropped something. Imagine being called into school to explain, 'Mrs Betty, I am sorry. It is I who says fuck.'

'Sweetheart. Let's be quiet for about ten minutes.'

'I don't want to be quiet.'

It was the child's right to have desires. It was part of her development to practice speech, but Tarisa could not help thinking, *Puck. Puck you, Mia. Puck you for how much you love to talk, although I know it's good for your development, although everyone tells me I should appreciate it now before you turn into a teenager and never want to talk to me again. But right now, I am tired, Mia. I am tired because I've been a mother for three years; I am tired just thinking about what this afternoon will be, with Barbies, with questions. I am tired because who I am, when you're not around, is a person content to just look at the view in the window. I do not like being forced to talk. I just want to be alone.*

They were cruising down the road, out of the tunnel. Tarisa watched the Merlion spit water into the bay. She thanked the tourists for reminding her that she lived in a neighbourhood that people the world over travelled to come and see. She pretended to tip a hat, making sure Mia couldn't see the gesture.

'Mom, what are you thinking?'

'Just looking at the tourists. You see the tourists?'

'Where?'

'There, here, all over,' she pointed, swinging her finger around at the packs of people.

'Where?'

'Here! Mia, they're all over!'

'Where?'

'Like, here!' she said, as they were already sliding into the neighbourhood of office towers.

'I don't see them.'

'That's because we've just driven by them.'

Mia tried to crane her neck back. 'Where are they?'

'Behind us.'

'I can't see them.'

'It's too late, Mia.'

'Why is it too late?'

'Mia, you don't stay on a bridge forever. If you want to see something while you're on it, you better catch it fast. Left here, please,' Tarisa instructed the driver.

'Wow! Live right here, ah?' he asked, craning his neck towards their tower, giving it a fuller look with eyes rising to absorb the lobby's high ceiling.

'Yes.'

'Expensive, ah?' he said as two security guards eyeing the approaching car came into view.

'A little. Thank you.' She waited for the car to come to a complete halt, then jumped out and headed to Mia's side to unbuckle her.

The concierge opened the glass double doors for them when Mia's feet had settled onto the floor. Tarisa greeted her with a smile and told Mia to say hello. She didn't.

The lobby's black marble floor was stained. Dull spots grew where acid that no one could see, ate away the surface.

She tapped her key fob onto the elevator panel and turned to make room for Mia, who liked to be the one to press 42.

The elevator doors opened midway on the floor with the pools and barbecue pits. Tarisa greeted the building manager who came in and smiled sweetly at them both.

'Building still half empty?' she asked, making conversation in Singlish she had learned from her former colleagues.

'Yes, ma'am.'

'How much again for a three-bedroom with one five two eight square feet?'

'For one five two eight'—the size of the apartment they were renting—'depending on the floor, but about three million plus plus.'

She was nowhere close to having that in her personal bank account.

'That's why still half empty? Cannot sell?'

'Yes ma'am. So expensive cannot sell. You rent or bought, ma'am?'

'Rent. And sorry. Maybe should have said half full.'

'Half empty also fine, ma'am.'

Tarisa bobbed her head, noticing it never turned into a proper nod. 'Guess so. Either way.'

When they reached their floor, they left their shoes outside the apartment.

'Don't go into the neighbour's space,' Tarisa reminded Mia, who took her shoes off too slowly for Tarisa's liking, but, when she thought about it again for a split second, that was fine, too. It meant less time together in the actual home.

CHAPTER 2

Tarisa closed the heavy door behind Mia, then swung around to the kitchen, looking briefly at the painting of a lion's face—fiery, its mane like the sun's. She had bought it in Phnom Penh during her last year of work, while she was at the World Economic Forum's ASEAN Conference—a place where many crooked, but important, men go. She was not proud to be among those humans but felt a tickling pride whenever she could include the conference in her resumé. Her sense of its importance might have been misinformed though. Because even after including it, she had never gotten any new jobs after becoming a mother.

She took an onigiri from the fridge, one that she had bought from a 7-Eleven, and unwrapped it, touching only the seaweed to avoid glutinous fingers. Scrubbing her hands would be another minute of doing something that did not interest her.

'You want your food cold, right, Mia?'

'Yes!' Mia shouted from the couch. The open plan kitchen let Tarisa easily hear her. The living room balcony door was open, putting the Singapore Strait into clear view, a view that confirmed the existence of both money and privacy.

They had no television. The one they had brought from DC years ago had blown up one day, belching loudly but leaving no broken pieces, no debris. A need to replace it had never arisen, conveniently, for they had not wanted Mia to walk by a temptation several times a day.

Tarisa didn't look to see if Mia was now staring at the ceiling or looking out into the water, although she knew that Mia was too young to realize that the backdrop of her childhood was privilege.

Tarisa washed and chopped the heads off a handful of strawberries with tap water, eyeing the fruit-wash solution that Chris had bought. She realized she had been forgetting to use it. She put the berries in a colourful bowl. *I'm poisoning Mia with pesticide.* She imagined what she would do now if the child disappeared.

Work. A crisp white button-down. A smile in the office pantry.

She imagined all the mothers who bought only organic fruits for their children.

They would never make this mistake. I bought the right popcorn today, but I forgot about the pesticide.

'Let's play Barbie, Mom,' Mia said from the other end of the home.

But she's here, really here, still here. And I do find her cute.

'What about food? I just washed strawberries.'

'Later.'

Tarisa looked at the clock hanging on the wall in the living room, midway between her and Mia. It was only eleven. She looked at Mia, who was staring at her for an answer.

'Fifteen minutes.'

'How long is fifteen minutes? Is it shorter than ten?'

'No, Mia, fifteen is longer than ten.'

'Okay, then fifteen minutes.'

Tarisa looked at the clock again and began the timer in her mind. She plopped the bowl of strawberries by the sink and looked at their innocent, sweet shape.

Four strawberries. With pesticide.

She clawed them into her grasp and inhaled them into her mouth, pushing until her palm touched her lips. Crushing them with all of her teeth, her eyes popped with the moisture of their sweet, acidic juice bursting along her gums.

Four strawberries. With pesticide.

She began her first step away from the sink, resisting the centre of gravity she felt there, pushing herself to walk towards Mia. She swallowed the strawberries that would now look like unidentifiable pink morsels in her throat, if anyone ever opened her up, right here right now. One foot landed, and with a deep breath she took another, taking her time to inch towards her child.

Take at least a minute to get there. Then you could argue you'd be left with fourteen to play.

Tarisa dressed up a doll until it became what Mia considered beautiful. Its short dress was floral and lacey; its hair fanned out like a peacock's plumes. Tarisa felt the need to summon empathy immediately—she could not love the way this doll looked, so dressed up in conventional citations of youth and beauty, but Mia's world was, clearly, a machinery of absorption rather than of critique. Mia was too young to know that what she saw as great was also a source of questions.

'Mommy, when you and Dad married, did you wear like this?'

'No, sweetie. We didn't have a wedding party. We just got married. I wore a simple dress. It was six dollars.'

'Why you didn't have a party?'

'We didn't see the point. We can love each other without the party. Like the way we love each other now. Daddy and I look happy together, right?'

'Yeah!'

'You can see it?'

'Yeah!'

'How?' She wondered if the rift between them was truly invisible.

'Kiss, kiss.'

Although she knew that the marriage was lacking, she tried to convince herself that it was lovely. 'Yeah. And there's more, you know. Like how he takes care of us. You and me. How he doesn't go and have another family.' She could hear herself trying to prove something to herself, not Mia. 'Some men do that, and they don't even tell their kids and their wives. Daddy also doesn't hit us. Some men do that too. They hit their kids and their wives.'

'Why they do that?'

'A lot of times, they do it when they're drunk. I don't know if it's *because* they're drunk.' She had not expected to have this conversation with Mia, but now she was listening to the things bubbling out of her mouth.

'What "drunk"?'

'Drunk is when people drink this thing, a very bad drink, called alcohol. Then they do all sorts of things they can't control or even remember.'

'Daddy drinks alcohol?'

'No, Daddy doesn't drink alcohol. That's what I'm trying to say. He's a good man. That's why I love him.' She thought of what she had seen in a parking lot in Uzbekistan, where she and Chris were vacationing, leaving baby Mia in Thailand with grandparents for a parenting break a year ago. A man was squeezing a woman's neck in the backseat of a car. He scraped her cheeks with his claw-like nails from his other hand. He gave Tarisa a dirty look when he saw her looking. She said nothing. Chris hadn't even seen what happened, he would later tell her.

Mia's Barbie came to a still. 'Me too. I love Daddy.'

'We both love him.'

'When I grow up, I want to marry Daddy.'

'Why's that?'

'I love him.'

'I know you do, sweetheart, but you can't marry him.'

'Why?'

'Because you should marry someone with whom you can have children, if you, or you both, want children. You can't make children with Daddy. It won't work that way.' She thought about the meaning of this sentence, which she, as witness to his impotence, understood in more ways than one. Tarisa moved the Barbie in her hand and tried to ventriloquize, 'You can't make children with Daddy. It won't work that way.'

'Me?'

'After you, no more.'

CHAPTER 3

'It's been fifteen minutes. No, seventeen! You got two whole, extra minutes!' Tarisa tried to sound happy. She stood up, already feeling she had mentally left the pretend-play. 'Come, let's clean up, sweetheart.' When Mia didn't move, Tarisa tried to sound more enthusiastic. 'Let's clean up!' She walked away, hoping that by leaving, she would help Mia feel the urgency of the task.

She walked to the kitchen and picked up her phone on the counter. She quickly googled why mothers are so tired. She couldn't understand her state, given she slept eight to ten hours every night. Before she could read what Google said, Mia was already crying for help.

Tarisa walked over to put the Barbie clothes back where they belonged. Then she walked back to the kitchen and transferred the onigiri to the dining table. She watched as Mia chomped away. She returned to the refrigerator to make herself a sandwich. She piled unevenly mashed avocados and smoked salmon pieces onto a slice of sourdough. She skipped the sandwich spread. She took her plate to the dining table, seated herself diagonally across from Mia, though the seat opposite from Mia was free, and gnawed through the dryish food, a tastier version of which she could imagine.

She considered calling Leela, who could also entertain the child. They FaceTimed regularly (though only when Mia was around), but Tarisa suddenly remembered Leela would be busy today. Tarisa had judged what that might mean, considering Leela had no job or friends. *Perhaps she wants to think that she's busy. Perhaps being able to say that she is busy gives her a sense of mattering somewhere.*

'After this, you wanna watch *101 Dalmatians*?' she asked Mia as soon as she realized Leela would not be available.

101 Dalmatians was the only cartoon that Tarisa could find in full on YouTube. She hadn't wanted to introduce Mia to Netflix, afraid that it would lead to regular pleas for cartoons on demand. YouTube, she thought, though she wasn't sure, was slightly more controllable since the home screen didn't show many possibilities all at once, and there was less of a sense of endless scrolling. As unfulfilling as it felt to engage with her child, Tarisa also did not want Mia to engage with Netflix by default. Netflix-fed children often looked as if they were struggling to engage with real life, as if they wanted to live in the screen.

On days like this day, when she knew she wouldn't last another four hours as an entertainer, she wanted *101 Dalmatians* to rescue her. Tarisa walked to the laptop on the coffee table and typed '101 Dalmatians' into the YouTube search bar. She looked at the time stamp to see how long the video would last. 1:28:09. She subtracted two minutes from the opening credits, which she would fast-forward over.

She would feel too guilty leaving Mia in front of a screen for those. She reminded herself that she needed to deduct time for the end credits too. So, in total, she would have one hour and twenty-four minutes to herself.

CHAPTER 4

'Mommy! Can you come watch with me? Please!'

'What's wrong, honey?'

'It's scary!'

'What?'

'The woman!'

'Cruella?'

'Yes! Mommy, come! Mommy!' Mia left the couch and ran towards her mother, who had left the coffee table immediately after pressing play, and was now standing at the kitchen sink, watching water drip. 'Mommy, come!' She tugged Tarisa's dress.

Tarisa had not expected Mia to still be afraid of Cruella. This was her third time watching the movie. The repetitions should have acclimatized her. 'Why are you scared when you know what she will do and how this will end?' She paused. 'This is not a rhetorical question.'

Tarisa herself recalled the unfolding of this scene: Cruella came to try to buy the puppies, Anita and Roger refused to sell, Cruella cachinnated until all one could pay attention to might be the length of her throat or the breadth of her lips. *Yes, perhaps it was a little unusual and such laughter might cause a little trembling, but all of that would soon end within a minute.*

'I don't know, Mommy. Come!'

Tarisa held Mia's hands. 'Okay, so we'll watch it together?' She pulled Mia's body close. 'We'll watch it together. You'll be fine.' Tarisa turned around to glance at the clock. It was only one. The remainder of this cartoon would buy her one more hour. Then there would be another three before Chris would come home. He would be home at ten past five, predictably. *Always reliable, so that I don't go crazy.*

'I'm scared, Mommy.'

'It's only a cartoon, sweetheart.' She lay on the couch and closed her eyes. Without meaning to, she began to fall asleep.

'Mommy, watch with me.' Mia shook her.

Tarisa patted her back to let her know that she was still there.

When Mia had calmed down, Tarisa tried to close her eyes again. Her eyelids folded without resistance. She heard a familiar scene. Anita—frustrating, little Anita—crying to Roger, who had gotten rid of Cruella and saved all the puppies from being sold, 'Oh, Roger, you were magnificent, darling!' Tarisa could visualize the scene. Anita was wrapping her arms around Roger, rubbing her cheek into his proud chest.

CHAPTER 5

Was it odd to like being alone so much, especially in the context of being a mother? She remembered Susan Cain's TED Talk, Cain wondering why, in the spirit of community, camp needed to be rowdy. Wasn't having a family just like being in camp? Mothers could be entitled to the silent 'animal warmth' of other people's presence, surely? Mothers need not be outgoing and chatty with their child.

Tarisa felt least agitated and most comfortable, loved, and capable of giving love, when Chris, Mia, and she were in the same room, living separate lives. She would sometimes feel words carving out an excruciating hole in her, if she had to talk. Talking did not energize this woman. She couldn't remember what did.

When Chris opened the door at ten minutes past five, his presence blew into her like a breeze.

'Hey,' she said. She dropped the coloured pencil, which fell from her hand like a bird dropping from a branch, and stood up. She had been fully awake for the past two hours: *101 Dalmatians* had ended, she had been rolling clay, colouring, cleaning up. Most of the movie saw her switching between catnapping and forcing her eyelids open, depending on when Cruella appeared.

'Hi, T.'

Hi, T.

She heard his voice echoing in her head, more like a gong than a whisper. It mattered, resoundingly, that he was there. He dove into the spot she had just left, replacing her. As she switched out, she glanced at his watch. Yes, it was eleven minutes past five. He had opened the door at five ten, exactly.

She deliberated whether to touch him. *Just lightly, on his tummy or shoulder.* A small touch would have warmed the tone of her greeting, which she saw as a miniature opportunity to convince herself that her marriage, underneath its outmost efficiency, still contained, on her side, affection. Yet, she gave him a cursory smile, picked up her phone, and floated into their bedroom. He said nothing, and she did not turn back to see what happened of him, though, as she closed the door now, she guessed that he had assumed something focused, forward-looking, epic. *A medallion man for how he works and fathers.*

The one-seater sofa took her in. She semi-reclined, propping herself up on a pillow and leaving her feet on the ground. Then, feeling like a foetus occupying much less room than it had been allocated, she reangled, pulled up her legs, and filled the cushion with more of herself, neck and legs dangling over the sofa arms. Immediately, she placed her phone on her navel, going on Facebook to look for nothing but to drown herself out of her surroundings, as the commuters in the morning had done.

She heard the clicks of checker pieces outside. A few weeks earlier, Chris had taught Mia how to play, spurring her thirst for three games daily ever since. He alternated the overall winner with Mia every day, playing by some unsaid rule for balance and equality. She looked out the picture windows where the ships were, hungry but unexcited about entering the kitchen if she would be with them nearby. The sunset roared in orange, and she told herself to stare at the sky until it burned out to black.

***

The bedroom door opened, swinging in. Chris and Mia were on tiptoe, their shadows nowhere to be seen. Late evening seemed lazy in this way—it did not do the work of replicating contours of people, it seemed only an observer of things. Chris trailed behind Mia, pushing her lightly at her small shoulders, trying to engineer her trail directly towards the bathroom.

'Mommy!'

'No, Mia. We talked about it. Leave Mommy alone, please,' Chris said.

Tarisa did not say a word. She got up from the couch, patting Mia's head and flashing a fake smile to Chris on her way out to the kitchen.

There, she saw a clean island and shining dining table and heard the dishwasher running. They had helped themselves to dinner without her, and she did not mind.

CHAPTER 6

Her foot latched onto the soaked bathmat, swinging it around with her toes' tight grip, mopping up the water that Mia's wet body had trailed out from the shower into the sink area, just two hours earlier. Tarisa had made sure to firmly close the bathroom door, so that Chris could have as much darkness as possible for his sleep.

She undressed, looked at her stomach and enjoyed the lines of muscles briefly before quickly looking away. Knowing that her husband never even glanced at them, *the most useless abs in the world*, filled her with sadness. She walked through the shower area towards the bathtub, filling it halfway with blistering water. The thrill that she would feel something, anything, extreme made her able to look forward to the future ten or so minutes.

A spark burst through her foot when it touched the water, inflaming the skin she had barely thought about. Thinking forward to her shins, she told herself that an easier part would soon come. Kneeling, she let them down, dyeing them with heat.

Her buttocks softened into the water. The heat suddenly ejected her. She sprang up and let cold water run, giving in, and sank down again, living in too much heat while waiting. She began to feel beads of sweat crawling over her neck and the pores of her cheeks widening, as if to eat up her face and leave her a hole.

After the cold and hot had mixed, she felt comfort that allowed for play. She watched her long strands of pubic hair float up, patting their tips, cherishing the quick entertainment.

She wanted to do something not mindless but relaxing, resulting in a reach to the side table. She opened a book, Eiko Tanizaki's *A Companion*, which courteous algorithms had figured, after her purchase of a novel on a separation and the other histories living in her browsers, might be an object for appreciation. She had not shared it with Chris, unlike how she did the previous novel, although both portrayed a marriage's calm disintegration with spirited silence. If Chris could not appreciate a book for its story, clapping only for the rhythms of sentences, then Tanizaki's accomplishments would appear pea-sized to him. Tanizaki's sentences were not rhythmically savoury. There was nothing to listen to besides raw content.

She hadn't wanted to risk recommending the book to him and seeing him read a few pages then put it away. It hurt, each time that happened—and things like that had happened enough. Each time he did not appreciate a book that she did, she might say that he also did not appreciate the roads of her mind, or how it intended to decorate itself. Which, when given that he also did not play kindly with her body, made her feel like she was only an idea of a wife to him.

Anyone would think the same.

'A separation always saddens. No matter who began it, there becomes sadness merely in separating . . .' She remembered needing to pick up from this line, which she had been reading while eating supermarket sushi a few days earlier, before she knew that Mia was sick, or that young boys could cling onto helpers who clearly didn't love them, or that watching the sky burn to black could make however she grieved—*Was this what every day was?*—still beautiful. It reminded her of the disposable chopsticks she pulled apart to eat the cold, hard rice. *Connected they would come, but only separated would they work.* Although she wondered what good could come out of a separation, she had not recently suggested it. The idea of being together still seemed worth prolonging, for it was only sex that was missing—in fact, perhaps even only partially. She still wanted it, certainly.

There was only one person who needed to be fixed.

Mia was coughing. Tarisa still had not slept. She heard a sustained blast of a ship horn outside her window—a steady stream of deep, confident sound. She looked at Chris, whose blanket covered him from his foot up to his nostrils. Although she wanted to wake him up, thinking about the sex they had had in the middle of the night in DC, she knew that he now preferred to be disconnected until morning, and that there was nothing for her to do but be alone again, waiting for the next day with midnight.

She tried not to mention Chris' impotence to his face. She knew how much it hurt him—her empathy was due. Balding had caused him to pick up finasteride just before they had begun dating, and he was one of the ultra-unlucky ones whom it had crushed for eternity, moving lust permanently out of his mind. They had not had sex since the time Mia was conceived, when Tarisa had just turned twenty-five.

Her eyes scanned her surroundings now. They were not new; it was not the thought of finding something new that gave movement to her eyeballs. Rather, Tarisa did not know what to do with herself in the middle of the night when she lay awake like this. Staring into darkness, then at shadows on the ceiling and the walls, she looked at how shadows didn't reveal how pupils move or any details of the object of the silhouette.

The bedroom was irregular in shape—ten edges in all, some meeting at perpendiculars, others at acute angles. She began to see farther, into the splendour of the view—luxury cruises and Indonesia to the east, Sentosa to the south, the Westin to the north. All over the apartment were tall, wide windows, as if they were in a control room, monitoring the places that they saw from forty-two floors above. They soared over the skyline and were almost at the top of their building.

But for all that she had in this view, she could not feel true top-down control in her life. In some ways, this was a relief. Feeling like a shell of herself had become familiar, and therefore navigable. She was conscious of living in spaces in between control and release. She could not hold on for long to statuses, feelings, or decisions, her story being that this splendid apartment was not where she had intended to be anyway. If things had gone as planned, she would have been in her doctoral cap and gown in Boston around now. In recent years, May had become a month of spiralling nostalgia that never left her mind blank. It was nearly the end of the month, and she hoped it would soon end.

The ship horn stopped. She heard a woman's voice on the port's PA system, but she could not—could never—make out the words. She wondered often what the woman was trying to say and could not tell.

Tarisa saw a green lawn, herself smiling sitting on a foldable metal chair in a cap and gown. The memory finished, and regret swooped in, as Chris had done after he'd said 'Hi, T'.

Back when they had first arrived in Singapore, she should have been more assertive about what she wanted to do, as she noticed she sometimes was now—showing earlier this evening, for instance, that she owed nobody a conversation. Yet, five years ago, when the return to Boston had still been a living question, she did not understand that a woman had to fight. 'That October' happened as a result, giving her the start to this limping through her own life.

She still had trouble digesting the idea that their supposed stay in Singapore, which was supposed to last only one year while she applied for a doctoral spot at Harvard, had grown into a permanent modus operandi. 'Applying' was even only perfunctory. She had shaken over a deal with a professor who saw her potential while she was completing her master's.

'I know you've missed the deadline for starting the PhD this fall, but if you apply in the fall, you can come back the following year. I'd be happy to work with you,' the professor had said. To be handpicked for a doctoral spot at Harvard had exceeded her expectations, even of herself.

Her American student visa would not permit her to stay after the semester ended, but she also could not imagine going back to Thailand, whose polluted environment and traffic jams she found uninhabitable, no matter how much tourists could tolerate them. She called her then-boyfriend in Washington, DC, to tell him about the meeting: 'Chris, I have to go somewhere in between.'

'I'll go too!' he had replied right away.

The memory replayed in her mind like a movie. It continued to reel her in.

He had been so committed to their relationship, showering her with trust, generosity, and reliability for three years, that she hadn't been surprised. 'What about Singapore?' she asked, to reciprocate his courtesy. There, he would have work. There, it was possible for someone interested in economics to live.

For herself—and she could no longer remember from where, which now highlighted the harebrained navigation of her life—Singapore contained cleanliness, safety, and order. It was the kind of environment to desire, or at least, recall as a possibility.

As she named it, she felt the smallness of the country pop out of her lips and disappear, like a bubble that would float only briefly. The petiteness of the country felt just right for a year's worth of living.

'Singapore,' she whispered it to herself again, popping her lips a little more than necessary to let the 'p' go. She could imagine saying to friends, 'We spent the last year in Singapore,' speaking of it like a campsite that had involved seeing the end from the beginning. To highlight the transitory space that Singapore should serve, she would take on insignificant work, embarking on her last odyssey of professional trinkets before hunkering down in academe.

'Yeah, Singapore! Sounds good. I'll just take leave for a year. We can come back,' he said.

His enthusiasm filled her with joy. Her world was coming together as she had been trying to shape it from her early teenage years, when she had been asked in school or by her father what she wanted for her future. Nobody asked her about the more temporary, uncontrollable dreams that she experienced at night. People were more interested in 'dreams' to mean the kind that involved effort and intention, and so she learned to pay attention to those.

The next time they were together in DC, she watched as he applied for a job in Singapore. She liked knowing that Chris would be near and loved that he had the desire to make their being together happen. Proof that he found her important laid here.

He secured an interview by the end of the week. He buzzed the little hair that he had left into a short shrub to look good. (She hadn't known, then, that this hair was a site of ramifications for her.) Afterwards, she asked how Singapore looked on his screen. 'Like a wall. There was a man and there was a wall,' he laughed. She could not yet imagine how ironic this statement would become, just a few months later.

They packed their belongings into cardboard boxes and were left with the one object they couldn't move themselves: Chris' grand piano, which he had bought on a whim, with her blessing—she'd told him, 'If it makes you happy.' He called in professional piano movers. While they were dismantling the piano's legs one afternoon, Tarisa's phone flashed, 'Home, Bangkok'. She immediately answered, worried that Leela should call her while deep night was cloaking all of Thailand.

'Can I talk to you about something?' Leela's voice was cautious.

'Is everyone okay? It's 3 a.m. there.'

'It's about you and Chris.'

Tarisa turned to Chris and stretched her lips to the side, alerting him of a situation.

'You can't live together if you're not married.'

'What do you mean? We've been living together. I live in Boston three days a week, but the rest, I spend with him. You know that.' She floundered a little in the only language she and her mother shared.

'But that's you living together in America. In Asia, if you're going to live together, you need to be married. After all, we are Thai. Do it for us. Save our face. Our friends live in Singapore.'

'But they don't know me.'

'But they might know you.'

'Right. And they might also *not* know me.'

'Please.'

Tarisa sighed, annoyed at her mother's habitual lack of logic. From the fact that Leela had let this keep her up, Tarisa knew that this subject would not be easy to dismiss. She quickly considered the options, considering that marriage wouldn't cause any inconvenience, and it was something that she and Chris had been talking about as a milestone for their future anyway. The conversation with Chris should be easy. They both knew that they would marry at some point, and the wedding would be simple. They were already registered domestic partners at Chris' office (in order for him to be able to share his generous insurance policy with her, so that she could get Invisalign almost for free; braces had been too expensive for her family when she was younger).

'Chris, my mom says we can't live together in Singapore if we're not married. She's afraid her friends will find out.'

'We can get married,' he replied immediately, as if the answer were obvious. His dark eyes lit up. She had seen them that way when they first met. She had fallen in love with him then and was falling in love with him again now.

'You sure?'

'I'm sure.'

The piano movers carried the piano parts out of the apartment.

'Mom,' Tarisa returned to the call. 'Okay, we'll get married.'

The following week, they walked through Foggy Bottom to the Courthouse in downtown DC. The embassies in the area made her think of her childhood, back when she was following her father along from one embassy to another. She felt lucky to have Chris, who shared her cultural amphibiousness, wetting into and drying out of being Thai or American.

In addition to registering their marriage, there was a prenuptial agreement that Chris' father had asked them both to sign. Tarisa had never heard of such a thing, and when Chris explained it to her, she realized it was a way for rich families to guard their wealth, especially for the worst case of a divorce. She didn't see the issue with signing, for she wasn't after his money. On the document her signature went, the dot for her 'I' pressed swiftly onto the page, the way she'd turn a key to lock the door.

For lunch that day, they ate something a little more special: rabbit braised in red wine. The rabbit they got from a Mexican grocery store, where tacos were offered wholesale, and the red wine from Trader Joe's. They planned to have lunch with both of their families whenever they made it out to Bangkok, nothing grander than that, and when the trip would be, they weren't planning to know. The simple union was meaningful to both, who read in its modesty their ability to focus on the marriage, not the wedding.

'Hello, Husband,' Tarisa said playfully after they had cleared the dishes, the rabbit's taste already forgotten, wrapping her arms around Chris' neck. She began to shift her feet, mocking a first dance. They fumbled, as neither knew how one should go. 'Now I can have more than Invisalign?' Although she joked, she realized now that her smile belonged to him.

'I'm lucky to have you as my wife,' he replied, stepping on her foot, which she, by instinct, yanked away, while her lips pursed together for a wide, closed-mouth smile she felt emanated from her heart.

The piano arrived a month after they did. The veneer had partially melted. Cracks bled through the wood. This was nothing they had been warned about, nothing, apparently that could have been helped. 'The humidity on the ship,' the piano colour specialist explained while patting the dissembled pieces. 'I can try to fix it but cannot promise.'

Chris eyed the changes without saying a word. This was not what he had wanted, but he was happier with the piano than without, Tarisa knew. He would be able to focus on how the keys still made the right sounds, how the melody that he wanted to make, the primary reason he got the piano, was not destroyed.

'We got three bedrooms just for you!' Chris said, rubbing its legs. He had moved on.

'The other room's for random people who come by,' Tarisa said. 'Right?' She wasn't sure. He had chosen this apartment. She had given him the rights without questioning, since he, who earned much more, was paying for rent.

'Anything. A two-bedroom was just too small.'

'Right. I'm sure we'll have a use for it.' She left the piano man and Chris alone to talk.

From the day the piano took its place in the room, Tarisa barely entered it, having no use for the space herself.

Tonight, Tarisa rolled onto the mattress on the floor, where Mia was sleeping. She caressed Mia's soft cheeks and thought about how Mia would be right now if she were raised by a helper who yelled or pinched her, as she had seen the woman with the Thanaka powder do less than twenty-four hours ago.

Mia shifted, flinging a leg onto her mother's thigh. Tarisa removed it, turned over, and closed her eyes. For another hour, maybe two, she found herself keeping awake, appreciating the stillness of the night. She wanted to be present with the silence.

She started noticing her mind emptying, no new thoughts coming, free association leading nowhere. She was now both hungry and ready to sleep. She walked into the kitchen and opened the refrigerator, searching for crackers. They were cheap, quick carbohydrates that could put her out fast. She didn't want to go down the road of sleeping pills. One pill might lead to another, and then, knowing how strong her desire to escape from reality could be, she was afraid of losing herself to something more.

Tarisa found crackers behind grapes and cherry tomatoes, which she used to feed Mia healthy food while she reserved the junk for herself. She turned around to the kitchen island and opened the drawer to find chopsticks.

She didn't want to touch the crackers with her fingers and then have to wash her hands in the middle of the night. The water would jolt her. She wanted to keep this serenity.

There were no chopsticks to be seen.

She tore a piece of paper towel off the holder on the countertop, then folded it in half to use like a pincer. One at a time, she dropped the crackers into her mouth until she felt a small knot in her throat. Perhaps she was gobbling too quickly. It seemed she had forgotten how to eat slowly. She thought about her meals for the past year: breakfast and lunch taken in a rush before drop-off and pick-up at school; dinner taken in a rush before the cleaning of the kitchen.

She looked on the rest of the island for anything else that she wanted to eat, but there was nothing. She gently elbowed the bedroom door open. She had left it slightly ajar, so that the sound of it opening and closing wouldn't disturb Chris. She drifted back into the cold air-conditioned room, feet never fully lifted from the parquet floor, so that her footsteps wouldn't wake Chris up. She checked to see if her snacking had woken him. He was still cocooned in his comforter, which he had pulled up to his nostrils, as usual. His eye mask and earplugs were both still intact. She leaned in closer to the crown of his head, where he had filled up some empty patches through follicular unit extraction and applied hair-growth serum every night, and sniffed. It strengthened her sense of connection with him, even though she couldn't say that she liked the smell, like pine and butterscotch.

She thought about whether to sleep on the bed next to him or to go back to the twin mattress with Mia. Tarisa remembered Mia's thigh slam from earlier and made her decision. She stayed on the bed next to Chris, smelling the clean sheets, which their weekly cleaner had just put on that morning. Thinking ahead, she let an arm out to dangle over Mia's mattress, leaving it for her to grab without having to call 'Mommy'—if she ever needed Mommy's comfort.

Before she could fall asleep, there was a child's cough.

Tarisa opened her eyes and rolled to the edge of the bed to look. Mia's lips were parted. She looked as though she was chewing and swallowing her phlegm bit by bit. There was the sound of saliva clicking with her gums, something like water droplets falling in a cave.

Mia is cute. Tarisa could imagine saying this sentence aloud. It wouldn't be the most natural thing to say, but rather, something she would say as if agreeing to a statement made by someone else. She had noticed how she sounded when she really thought Mia was cute. In those moments, she would say, 'She's *so* cute,' flooding that 'so' with emotions that she thought were otherwise ineffable. But, at this hour, she managed only 'Mia is cute', a sign of, even to herself, half-hearted adoration. She couldn't tell what didn't make it fuller.

Mia coughed again and rolled over. Tarisa looked at her body that was now turned to face the bay window. Tarisa climbed down into the space that Mia had just made and put her hand on Mia's blanket-wrapped belly. She looked again at her child. The small parting of the curtains allowed moonlight to illuminate her tiny nose, a soft mound in the centre of her face. It was the part of her that looked the most incompletely formed, and it reminded Tarisa of what the little girl had looked like in ultrasounds. She touched Mia's nose and kissed her cheek. 'I love you.'

Mia's cough grew louder and steadier. It became clear that her body badly wanted to expel the phlegm, but she swallowed. No matter how many times they had told her she needed to help her sick body get the germs out, Mia didn't listen.

Chris shot up in the bed, pulled his ear plugs out, and lifted his eye mask up slightly. They both started towards Mia's water bottle, which they had asked her to leave on the bay window. 'Oh,' they both said, when their hands overlapped. He lifted his eye mask up fully now. His half-closed eyes acknowledged Tarisa through a squint.

'I got it,' Tarisa said clearly.

'Thanks,' he mumbled. He returned the eye mask to half-mast, and they both walked back to sit together on Mia's mattress. She had woken up. Without their help, she propped herself up. She began to cry—a sudden, vehement blast of sound.

'Have a sip of water, sweetie,' Tarisa said, holding the bottle in front of her.

'Yeah, you should really have some,' Chris echoed.

Mia didn't take the bottle immediately. She looked at it for a few seconds, still in tears. Tarisa was afraid that Mia would push it away, which would make her even more frustrated. But Mia finally reached out with one hand, and then the other.

'Look at her now.' Tarisa smiled at Chris. She turned to Mia and caressed her black hair. 'You're a big girl, Mia. When you were a baby, you couldn't do this.'

Mia liked stories of when she was a baby. This one drew her out of her crying.

'When I was a baby, what did I do?' she asked.

'We'd try to wake you up to drink some water, and you'd just cry and cry.'

'Today I'm a big girl?'

'To*night*,' Tarisa emphasized the correction, 'you're a big girl. Good job.'

Mia sipped some more water, proud. Then her lips let the straw go.

'After this can you sleep with me, Mommy?'

Tarisa looked at the child, inhaled, and didn't answer for a few seconds. 'Sure, sweetie. Of course, I can.'

Mia held the bottle out to signal that she was finished. Chris took it from her. Tarisa pulled her own blanket down from their bigger bed.

'Mommy, I love you,' Mia said. Then, she coughed, her back turned towards Tarisa. 'Daddy, I love you,' she added. She coughed again, more strongly this time.

Tarisa suspected something. She snuck her hands around Mia's waist to prop her up, and sure enough, what she feared was coming fast.

'Chris, trash can!'

Her hands, frozen around Mia's tummy, were coated with vomit.

'Should I carry her to the bathroom?' he was alert now, his eye mask on the top of his head again.

They had established a routine for Mia's vomiting: Chris would clean Mia up while Tarisa replaced the bedsheets and headed for the laundry machine in the kitchen to wash the soiled ones right away.

'Wait,' she said. Her hands were still locked around Mia's tummy.

'Okay, I wait.' Whenever he was trying to be a good teammate in urgent situations, he would regress to the most rudimentary grammar, locking in to receive commands.

She noticed that she had put him on high alert. 'Thanks. Just wait. I'm just trying to get a sense first of how far the vomit has gone, like what it's touched.'

With the lights still off, she could see only what the moonlight allowed. There seemed to be a patch of wetness right below her knees in the centre of the mattress, but nothing on the blankets or pillows. Mia stood in her mother's grip, blubbering from the shock of the vomit shooting out of her.

'Okay, now you can take her,' Tarisa continued. Chris hoisted her away to the bathroom as Mia kicked and cried. He tried to stabilize her in his arms so that her vomit wouldn't fly onto their furniture.

Tarisa lifted the clean blankets off and piled them onto the queen bed. She bundled up the bedsheet and pressed it along with the mattress protector into the washer. Already, she could hear them in the bathroom. 'Daddy, I'm cold! I'm cold! I'm cold!'

'Please, Mia. Please! I'm just trying to help you!'

'I'm cold! I'm cold! I'm cold!'

'Mia, please just appreciate the fact that you have someone to clean you,' Chris tried to reason. 'Augustine doesn't.'

He was referring to a child Mia had met only once: the daughter of their cleaner's neighbours, whom the cleaner had brought along one day because the girl's parents were nowhere to be found. She had become a convenient point of contrast for Chris, who liked to use Augustine to remind Mia of her own privilege.

In the kitchen, Tarisa scrolled the washer command to 'Hygiene' and began the cycle. 'Mix' could have been enough, but she didn't want to leave any trace of vomit to chance. She didn't like the idea of stains, which made her shiver. She imagined people in the family walking around, propagating germs and leaving splotchy marks. She was unable to pinpoint the start of this repulsion, but she recognized the image that frequently appeared in her mind: a trail of festering organisms she did not desire in her space. Her need for cleanliness had only started after Mia's birth.

She waited for the sound of the water hitting the bedsheets. From inside the bedroom, Mia's voice became louder and louder. Tarisa put her hands to her ears, pressing so much that she started to hear a high-pitched, discomforting note. Without more to do there, she returned to the bedroom, despite despising the noise.

She heard the child's bawling and wanted to stop it. She turned to the bathroom. Mia was in the shower, naked behind the frameless, toughened safety glass screen. Chris sat on a plastic stool under the rain shower, hosing her down with the detachable showerhead. The bathroom was lit only by the moonlight coming in through the bay window next to the bathtub. Chris had left it slightly ajar. It's what their cleaner had suggested they do, to get rid of the drain flies.

In the window behind them, the Sentosa skyline lit up. Chris hadn't closed the hinged shower door. *Good. I would do the same. Let the noise out.* She was grateful that Chris took the duty of cleaning Mia. Their tasks usually took the same amount of time, but the ones that she preferred were those less directly involved with the child.

Chris must have kept the lights off because he was afraid of becoming fully awake and not being able to fall back to sleep.

However, to Tarisa, showering a child screaming 'I'm cold!' in what must have been scary darkness seemed moronic, as if you were asking for more work for yourself: first, having to listen to the child's screams; then, having to calm the child down. Without asking Chris, she hit the light switch and asked if she could help.

Mia stopped crying when she saw her mother standing at the threshold, but soon went back to it.

'Of course you're cold. We're in an air-conditioned environment,' Tarisa said.

It was a familiar scene. She eyed the countertop to see if Chris had already brought in a change of clothes and where he put her soiled ones.

The soiled clothes were next to the drain, soaking. *Good.*

'And after this, I'll brush your teeth, too,' he said to Mia. Tarisa wanted to ask if that was necessary, but she realized his extra effort wouldn't be her problem.

Tarisa switched on the bedroom lights and turned to the closet to look for a new mattress protector. They had bought some during a vacation in Australia, where the K-Marts and Targets, which didn't exist in Singapore, made her explode with joy. She had never used mattress protectors until Mia came along. Now that they had become an important part of life, Tarisa was excited whenever she found them cheap. She seemed to have gone overboard in Australia, she realized, seeing a few unopened boxes in the closet. There would be no second baby—a decision that she and Chris agreed on, and that his impotence was supporting—so these mattress protectors might keep sitting in the closet. Or, Tarisa had thought once or twice, she could donate them to the families that needed them more. *Families like Augustine's.*

She wrapped Mia's mattress up with a new mattress protector and fitted a clean grey sheet over it. All the sheets in the home were grey. Mia, who had been kept from seeing children's bedding in shops, did not know that it was unusual for a child of her age to be sleeping on a slab so much like a marble chopping board. The grey matched with the steely look Tarisa had given the rest of the home.

They came out of the bathroom. Chris, as usual, had dried Mia's feet with a towel, afraid of her slipping on the marble bathroom floor. On their bed, he changed her into new diapers, pulling out the cuffs as Mia lay kicking and screaming a different refrain now: 'I'm sleepy! I'm sleepy!'

'I know! I know! But we have to do this! I'm doing this because I love you! Think about Augustine!' he said.

Tarisa stayed quiet for as long as she could, looking for another task. When it was clear that there was nothing else that immediately needed her attention, she went to stand next to Chris, both parents peering down at the child.

'I'm sleepy! I'm sleepy!' Mia continued to kick and scream. Tarisa turned to look at the clock. *Four a.m.*

'Do you think she'll go to school? Should we keep her home?'

'I think she can still go,' Chris replied. His hands tried to yank the last bits of the diaper cuffs out.

'I'm asking because if we think she won't go, then we need—'

'I'm sleepy! I'm sleepy!'

'Mia, we're trying to talk!' Tarisa snapped. She wanted to show Chris her fatigue. She had never been such a conscious performer until Mia came along. There were so many ways that she was at the end of her rope and wanted to prove it to Chris, to justify why she had become so much colder and more silent these past few years.

'I'm sleepy! I'm sleepy!' Mia said.

'Mia, we're discussing this because of you! For you! What were you saying?' Chris continued to scrub the child with a towel, but Tarisa knew the question was directed at her.

'I was saying—'

'Mommy, I'm sleepy! Daddy, I'm sleepy!'

'Go ahead. Please, continue, T.'

Against the backdrop of Mia's repetition, Tarisa stressed each word, closing her eyes. 'I was saying! If she's not going to school—'. She inhaled. She opened her eyes and looked at Chris, still focused on the task of the diaper. 'We need to turn the alarm off! Try to sleep more! Get some more rest!' she shouted, trying to be heard over Mia's cries.

'I'm sleepy!'

'Mia, please. We're almost done.' Chris maintained his polite language, despite his knotted brows.

'But I'm sleepy!'

The second hand of the clock was gliding silently, effortlessly, past one mark then another.

'But I'm sleepy!'

Tick, tick, tick.

'Mommy! I'm sleepy!'

Tarisa looked away from the clock and peered into her daughter's eyes. 'Mia, stop it,' she said. 'You fucking puked on yourself.'

She had been conscious enough to say it quietly. She told herself every time she did it, that she would stop cursing at Mia, even if barely audibly. There was no way that it could be good for her growth. Chris had already told her that he didn't like his daughter being cursed at by her own mother.

This time, however, he seemed to empathize and said nothing.

'Mommy! Come sleep with me!' Mia yelled when Chris put her on the mattress.

'You can't order me around me like that!' Tarisa said, noticing that her inhibition of short profanities had diverted into longer huffs and puffs.

'Mommy!'

'Can you please say it nicely, Mia?' she groaned.

'Come sleep with me, please, Mommy.'

'Okay. Everyone, game over. Let's go to bed. Good night. Thanks, Chris. Have you said, "Thank you, Daddy"?'

'Thank you, Daddy.'

'Do you still need to vomit?' Tarisa said.

'No. Finished already.'

'Okay, let's go. Lights off. It's a school day. Right, Chris? That's what we decided? Give it a chance?'

Chris heard her subtext about the lights and went to turn them off. Tarisa had increasingly been giving him indirect orders. She felt guilty, undeserving of such a docile partner who fell into her trap each time. Yet, she could only continue to enjoy his help, imagining that without it, she would be left alone to do everything related to the child, while he would be nowhere near understanding the labour its dependence necessitated, and her efforts, struggles, and sacrifices would all go unnoticed. She wondered if his truckling idiosyncrasies were born from his guilt from 'that October'. Although, even if such were true and he was trying all the ways to make up for it, she could not classify this as compensation.

'So, the alarm's still on?' Tarisa asked.

'Still on,' he said.

'That's good. It's better if she goes to school.'

<hr />

Tarisa heard Chris sit back onto the bed and guessed the rest of this creature of habit's actions—he brought both his legs under the comforter, let his back down onto the bed, and cordoned off two senses with his eye mask and ear plugs. From the mattress she was sharing with Mia, Tarisa turned to check, and her guesses were true.

Mia, on the other hand, was wrestling incessantly with her blanket, flailing around in the dark, as if the night did not yet deserve a conclusion. Tarisa put a pillow in between them, hoping to block off her kicking, but that pillow only contracted her own space.

'Can you stop that kicking please? Or else I'll have to go sleep on the bed with Daddy,' she asked Mia as she slid off onto the parquet.

'Why, Mom?'

'Because I can't—' she bit her lips to stop a profanity from exiting. 'Because I can't sleep when you're kicking me,' she tried again.

'Okay, sorry, Mom,' Mia said, stopping her legs. She turned to gaze into Tarisa's eyes and beneath her own, as if unthinkingly, formed a slow, settled smile, which had an immediate effect, petrifying Tarisa's frustration.

Tarisa watched Mia's sleeping body breathe, swelling and deflating. It was cute when a small body attempted something as grand as breathing. 'Cute' was the only word she could think of, confusing herself with her inability to produce more adjectives to use with Mia. Some people—mothers whom she had met when the kids were infants in the same swimming class—told her teasingly that she described her child clinically. Tarisa didn't know how else to do it. *My emotions are either clinical or ineffable.*

What she didn't try to put into words tonight was how she watched Mia's chest while thinking about the little heart that she had created. She remembered the first day that she heard Mia's heartbeats through the prenatal ultrasound. The sound, which reminded Tarisa of suction or making bubbles underwater, put tears in her eyes. She was unashamed to show the doctor her act of crying, which kept to a body so still, as if the tears had to free themselves out of an out-of-sync environment.

At home, knowing that two hearts were beating inside of her, she and Chris talked about a baby who would inch itself up to stand on their legs, patting its small, fat hands all over their laughing faces. A heavily pregnant Tarisa climbed onto Chris' lap one day and pretended to paw his face lightly like she imagined their future baby would.

Now, Tarisa let her hand move up and down Mia's belly, floating with her breaths. She thought about the elements of the night—a sick child, sleepy parents, someone puking, more people cleaning, everybody just falling back to sleep so that they could wake up and try to get to school on time the next day.

The faces of those mother-women—she didn't know if she should call them friends—came back. 'The way you talk about Mia is so funny!' Regina said over tea at a fancy hotel.

Regina, who lived largely alongside a helper, not husband, had four kids who enamoured her without pause. She taught them math daily, in two languages—one hour in

English, and then the same thing for an hour in Mandarin. Tarisa never knew how to even begin attracting that kind of energy for herself. She had a partner, a cooperative one, and still, she could barely manage.

A sick child in the middle of the night opened up time without the promise to close it back up. *There are women like Regina who would not view it so.* Tarisa realized that she had been listening to Mia's cries with the feeling of wanting to punch a broken record, while also remembering that some women, like Regina, were left to do all the tasks alone, from wrapping up the bedsheets, to washing them, to cleaning the child, to somehow making sure no more damage was done to the furniture. The child and its attached problems were theirs to deal with single-handedly while their partners often travelled in the name of work or slept through the chaos, claiming to do so, or being given a free pass to do so, in consideration of the following day's office travail. Then, after that—all the labour that amounted to martyrdom— these mothers would look forward to chitchatting with other mothers, arranging for breakfasts and coffees (which, Tarisa suddenly remembered, was something she needed to get back to Regina about, not expecting to feel complete happiness about their get-together until she could understand why talking would be fun). Maybe because of that, how they sometimes displayed themselves in public as still bodies and frothing lips, the public often did not regard them as having serious lives or a vocation.

She closed her eyes, hoping to sleep off how small she felt, and waited for the morning, but the one she wanted never came.

Around 5 a.m., Mia began to shiver, rattling like an egg let into boiling water. She did not seem conscious of it. *Febrile seizure?* Tarisa was afraid. She could not imagine this being the end of Mia and looked to her phone for advice and comfort.

'Shivering, according to the British National Institute for Health website, is normal for a feverish child. Do not go rushing to the doctor because of shivers,' she summarized to Chris. 'Non-governmental websites second: Please, don't.'

They considered paracetamol while their eyes were still glued to articles on their phones. Mia had never shivered like this, however. On this, they agreed.

'Let's just go to the hospital. I'll get the bags packed in case we want to stay overnight. These things are usually two nights, right?' Tarisa said.

'Right.' They were familiar with the process. Mia had also been in the hospital the previous year, after getting sick during vacation in Shanghai.

Tarisa slipped some diapers, pyjamas, and underwear into a weekend bag. She changed from Chris' boxers into Lululemon leggings. She knew that there was no need to look great at the hospital. She would need to look just comfortable and able to pay. She wasn't proud that her money came from Chris, but, when she needed to, she could deploy its benefits.

Ten minutes later, they were out the door, Mia still rattling, pressed against Chris' chest. They passed their neighbour's door. Tarisa eyed the glittery stilettos in front. He always used prostitutes. *Rich people who need to buy sex.* She imagined him sleeping with prostitutes while his little kittens meowed around them. She never told Chris what she sometimes imagined saying to him: *If only I were attracted to you, we could . . .*

She and Chris had not had sex for four years now. Chris' erectile dysfunction had turned into a total lack of libido. After Mia was born, they both thought that it was the fatigue of raising a new-born that stifled his lust. Rarely—once every three or four months—after she initiated, he would want to try, but he couldn't get hard. He would try to squish the lump of his limp package somewhere around her pelvis. She thought that it had the energy of a catapulted cotton ball, and while she felt unfortunate about the repetition of his ungainly, manic lust, she also didn't want to give up on her own sex life.

He had dismissed his wife entirely as an object of desire, and he noticed none of her heartbreak. It did not occur to him that her silence was a result of not only parental fatigue, but also the growing distance she felt with him. She had lost a romantic partner, and it was not enough for her to know that her daughter had a champ of a father while she was missing a more complete husband.

She remembered that line from Tanizaki's novel, which she had been reading just before the night's ordeal, about an unravelling marriage: 'He still loved his wife, but neither now excited the other. Their tastes and ways of thinking all still matched perfectly.'

Essentially, Tarisa had a roommate, one she considered to be very polite, hard-working, and thoughtful. He had changed so much—all for the better, aside from the impotence—ever since 'that October'.

There was a reason they were here, not according to her will.

The taxi now arrived at the glass double-doors of the lobby, ready to take them in. The concierge pushed a button to open the door for them. 'Thanks,' they said in unison.

'How's her shivering?' Tarisa asked.

'Less,' Chris said.

Tarisa opened the left car door for Chris, then got in on the right. It was the same thing every school morning, when Chris would put Mia in the taxi from the left, and she would go to the right and say while disappearing from his view, 'Thanks, Chris, I love you.'

Now, at just after 5 a.m., Tarisa sat in the middle and Chris took her usual spot. She felt grateful that he was there. She knew that she would need him the moment that Mia was awake again. Mia was slowly waking, the shivers leaving her. She would want to chat when she was fully awake, and Tarisa would not have the energy to entertain her alone.

'Stamford Hospital,' she directed the driver.

He accelerated into the night voicelessly. He did not seem the chatty kind.

CHAPTER 7

This was how dark it was the night they saw Singapore together for the first time. The sky was uneager to be electric. The bridge they had just crossed, despite being the longest in Singapore, still cut short. Its exit waited just after its entrance, like a parent eagerly standing at the gates of a preschool.

From being in one neighbourhood, often outlined by the shadows of tourists, they were now in another—more sedate and populated by jaded locals.

'Baby'—a memory floated to her as they paused at a red light. They hadn't yet had a real baby. She was still twenty-four; he was her baby. 'Could you help me proofread this statement of purpose whenever you have time?' she was saying, focused on her laptop screen, in that memory.

He didn't reply. She looked up and saw him shaking his head. Back then, there was much more hair.

'It's October. I've got to start working on it,' she tried.

She had expected him to help her. Her tongue rolled over her front teeth, pausing at her canine, when she realized he was not responding. This lack was new.

Just a couple of minutes ago, putting the last full stop on her statement of purpose, she had been imagining them back together where the rabbit was cooked in red wine.

'We're not going back,' he said.

She thought she had misheard him. There were two things in the world that she had never fathomed: that they would not go back, and that he would be sure of it. She thought she had heard both just now.

'Say that again?'

'I said we're not going back.'

The effect of this was like that of a heartbreak, except whereas heartbreaks happen over an extended period of time, all of the energy and grief of a heartbreak felt collapsed into a brief time frame, so brief that it hit like a whip, across her face and chest. She saw the life she had envisioned escaping out of her body.

'We came saying we'd return in the fall. Are you kidding?' She was not shouting. She found it hard to express how she felt, though the stillness of her own voice, its matter-of-factness, surprised her.

'I changed my mind,' he said.

He turned away from her. He let her study him. She moved the laptop away from her lap, felt her heart pounding underneath her shirt with the Harvard logo. He was wearing one, too. They had joked earlier in the day about looking like twins.

'Oh my goodness.' She heard her voice trying to shoot out, like a little baby sprout trying to surface in a thunderstorm. 'You planned this.'

He didn't reply. A chill reverberated in her chest.

He stepped back a few steps into the piano room, where he began to rearrange his sheet music. She stared at his nonchalance. What was happening? Many things looked the same—him in a t-shirt and boxers, glasses, somewhere near his piano, almost six-foot tall—but something had changed.

Suddenly, every piece of furniture seemed to have more weight. They were pieces of stone setting in.

Had he really known from the moment they had married that he was not going to return? (He still had not answered.) The answer to that question mattered. If she were to stay with her husband, the one she had married just two months ago, she, at least, wanted to hear that he had not planned this, that he had not foreseen whipping and wounding her. He couldn't have dared to marry her, bring her to a new country on her own gap year, and suddenly tell her that they were never leaving and that her gap year was never ending—could he? They both knew that she could adapt to new environments, but he wasn't as Machiavellian as this, was he?

'I don't know,' he said.

'You don't know what?'

'I don't know if I've been thinking about staying all along.'

'How the fuck could you not know?'

'Please don't say "fuck". There's no need to be rude,' he said, closing the piano room door and moving to load the dishwasher. She had never used the word before with him.

She went into the guestroom and slammed the door—the first of many slams that would punctuate the rest of their week. Within seconds, he was knocking.

'Can you please understand,' he began, 'that I really like Singapore, and we don't *need* to go back to America?'

'*I* need to go back to America. *I* need to go back to school.' She was sure of this word, 'need.' Using it felt no less natural than, 'I need to be who I am.'

'You don't *have* to go back to school,' he said.

'So, I'm supposed to stay here and do what, Chris? On this finance island, what am I supposed to do with my education degree? It's not even a teaching degree. It's a degree where I *study* education. It's a degree *for research*. I don't want to be a teacher in an international school, okay? I want to do research, and I want to be a professor! And I *can* be a professor! Julia invited me to be her student. *Julia Mac-fucking-Donald.*' She took a breath. 'I could teach in America! As a professor, a historian of education! You know it's what I wanted to be!'

'You don't *have* to teach in America—'

'*You* have an economics PhD from Yale. You can do and say whatever the fuck you want.'

'Please, stop saying "fuck". Please. And, you *already* have a job.' She could hear him wincing as he spoke, as if he were the underdog.

'My contract is for a fucking year! Because we were supposed to stay for a fucking year! And there's no fucking progress in it, that fucking job! I'm a food writer at a small, local, dying magazine. It's *intentionally* a gap-year kind of gig!'

'It doesn't always have to be about progress!' He paused and lowered his voice. 'We already have money. Can you please open the door?'

She did, staring at him. The features of his face, usually bright and open, looked leaden and scrunched.

'It's not about money. And this is *your* money. Going back is about what *I* want to do, for my own brain and future.'

'No, the money is ours. We're married. It's ours.'

'There's a prenup, Chris!'

'I don't care about the prenup! That was a show for my dad!'

She was quiet. He had always shared his money with her in the past—*that Invisalign and more.* He did not have to share anything with her, and yet, he constantly did. He probably wasn't lying about sharing more of it now. Not all married couples were financially generous with each other, but it was how her housewife mother and working father did it, too. A future like that for herself didn't seem impossible, if only because she had seen her parents treat money the same way.

'You have a brain. You have a future, here,' he said.

'But what about the ambition?'

'What?'

'I said, "What about the fucking ambition?" I don't *care* about the money, Chris. I want to go back to school. I've worked for this. You know my childhood didn't have opportunities like yours.' Her father had taught her to be ambitious, to reach for that PhD if she could. To him, academic ambition was a path to a better life, and on that path, she had learned what pride could come from ambition, what aliveness and self-respect she could feel when she was on top of her game.

'Ambition isn't everything. Ambition is very American.' He repeated, 'Ambition is very American.'

She felt like she'd been slapped in the face. His lowered voice, she was coming to understand, wasn't about him calming down to compromise. His mind was already made up. His voice had risen earlier because he was annoyed with her dreams, not because this was a real argument. He didn't see any argument to be had.

'Ambition isn't American. It's for people who have dreams,' she tried.

'Why do you need to dream? We have enough money. All of this—' his hands panned around the room—'is already real. Why do you have to dream *more*?'

'I told you it's *not about money!* It's what I want to do *for myself*!'

'Tarisa, we're not American. You don't have to keep on dreaming.'

No one had ever said this to her face. It had always been Tarisa who had had to tell other people, in an accent that seemed to contradict her message, 'Actually, I'm not American.'

'Culturally, I am quite American,' she said now. 'I lived there for a decade, Chris. My seminal years. You, too. I will dream all the fuck I want, have all the fucking ambition I want to have.'

'Not me!'

'Yes, you! You were there since you were fifteen! That's sixteen years, Chris. Connecticut! You were in *Connecticut*.'

'I'm Thai! And *you* are also Thai.'

She looked at him. Was he serious? Until now, she had always felt comfortable with the headspace that they shared, belonging to neither here nor there. 'I thought you understood me. When have I ever fit in with Thai people? What are you even saying? *You* don't even fit in with Thai people.'

'But we are Thai.' It sounded like a conclusion, like what Leela had said to her earlier, in her pleading for her and Chris to marry.

She bit her lips. 'Not any more than I feel American. I've never even been to a Thai school.'

'Whether or not you've gone to a Thai school is not the point. The point is,' he stressed, 'I would like to stay here, and we can stay here because we don't *have* to go back to America. Can't you understand that ambition doesn't have to exist? Look at my maids in Bangkok—'

Maids?

'—they don't ask for a better future. They joined our household when they were ten and they die happily as maids, and that's all life is! It doesn't need to be bigger and bigger.' He threw his arms out, jutting his head towards her in a way that looked mocking.

He had never looked so ugly. For the first time, she saw how lopsided his eyes were, how aggressive he could look, staring at her, waiting for her to yield. He cocked his head slightly to the side as if to avoid a blow.

It was the first time she'd heard his family's old money talking. She had a few friends, people descended from nobility and aristocracy, who sometimes showed sporadic tugs from their roots. They were so certain about where they were from, even if they had already seemed to drift away and spent more time abroad than in Thailand. She, from a middle-class family, never felt the moneyed pull of those roots. It was the essence of her being middle-class to constantly flow.

Alone again, after she had closed the door on him, she saw how what he said could be true. Being in America for middle school, then college and graduate school, didn't make her American. (What, then, would?)

It didn't take her long to begin processing what he had said. Her history, growing up here and there, seeing cultures differ and people adhere so firmly to their beliefs, even if, on the other side of the world, nothing similar was fathomed, made her see the absence of anything absolute.

Images whirled through her mind, of people pulling away and reconstructing pieces of her body. There had been her mother telling her that she needed to be married to live with Chris because that's what Thai people would do. Now, there was him telling her that she wasn't American, even though she felt so at home in DC. She had always thought of her flexibility as amphibiousness, a quality that allowed her to adapt without attachment, but now she realized that to others, her flexibility was their convenience.

'We just got married. Are we already looking at divorce?' she asked, seeing it as a rational solution.

'No, no divorce!' he said from the other side of the door.

Alone, she sat in the guestroom, numb and confused. She looked out into the water and the sparkling cruise ships as they came in and docked—a world that went on, no matter what happened to her. It could move on as if she didn't exist.

She had never felt this way, never been so upset at Chris, but maybe that was because she had never known this side of him. Maybe she had never actually known this man. She wasn't sad seeing the stranger as much as she was grieving the loss of the man who had disappeared.

The following morning, when they met in the living room, she tried to find her old Chris, the one who shared everything with her. She looked to see where he was in this man's body. They looked so similar, dressed so similarly, carried themselves so similarly, that she was sure her Chris was in him.

She pleaded her case again, but the conversation turned into the same argument. This man in front of her was adamant—so adamant that she insisted again upon divorce, but he repeated, 'No, no divorce!' shaking his head as if her idea were foolish.

'Then, I go, you stay here, and we stay married.' This option was also obvious to her, she, who realized now that her life, which she often associated so much with her mind, was now just as much a product of her body, and her body was being told it could not move from Singapore.

'No, no long-distance marriage either!' he shouted, annoyed.

'Then what do you even mean? What options do you see for *me*?' If there was anything that was the opposite of an out-of-body experience—a word that would equally emphasize how much it felt locked in to be in one's own body—this was the word that Tarisa would use now to explain how tethered she felt by her own flesh. 'We used to have a long-distance relationship. It wasn't a problem.'

'That was, *max*, DC-California, when you were at Berkeley for your first master's degree, not Boston-Singapore! Look, you have a job already! You don't *need* to change it!' He paused. 'How can we even *know* you'll stick to the PhD?'

He turned away from her. 'You didn't like your first PhD at Berkeley, so you stopped at the master's there. Now you say you'll attempt a second one.'

She ached listening to this. He didn't know that this was what she felt insecure about, but she did, and she felt it to her core. It was true: she had interests that constantly changed. She had dropped her first PhD in Comparative Literature, even when she was recruited as a high-potential student, a Fellow. Then, she had asked her professors for recommendation letters to law school, when she had thought she wanted to study law. And when she didn't get into the law school of her choice, she asked those same professors for recommendations again, for education school this time. Chris was right: she was a changer, and a changer who changed not when she *had* to, but because she wanted to. Was this ambition or just a bad habit? Could a person used to change since childhood grow into an adult unhealthily used to it?

She looked at his profile, wishing he would turn so that she could look him straight in the eye. She had no proof from her past that she could stick to something, besides him. He was her only constant. She thought about the professors she had left when they had been the ones to recruit her, giving her the fellowship to study for free, while every other student financially struggled to be a part of the programme. She imagined their opinions of her now: smart but unreliable, capable but capricious.

'Because this is what I really, really want. And it's what I'm good at. I'm good at research,' she replied. If she had to be honest with herself, there was no better or more honest answer. She didn't want to do anything as badly, nor did she feel as capable at anything else. To have somebody believe in her, Julia MacDonald, a professor she revered at Harvard, also made the difference.

A part of her, however, still entertained the thought that he might be right, but she didn't let him see it.

They tried to be normal in their interactions in the weeks after that conversation, sometimes even making love, but every connection, body or mind, felt like it ended with space withheld. Tarisa's ambivalence felt like ice and fire coursing through her veins at the same time.

A voice would tell her to cool down and see things from his perspective. Another voice would inflame her to fight again. Occasionally, she did, but he always tamped down her outbursts with the same response—he was enjoying it here; it was unnecessary to move back; how could they be sure, given her track record, that anything solid would come out of her dreams?

She would find out, only later, that this wasn't his real reason for wanting to stay.

CHAPTER 8

When Mia was no longer shivering, Tarisa thought about going home. *Overreacting could make one a silly mother.* She reached out to touch Mia's calf and held her hand there. She felt the stillness of Mia's muscles and bones. Despite this, she could not tell if Mia would shiver again. Or, worse—even though this might just be a common myth—enter a state of shock. Her mother had told her once something about sick children going into shock. She had never read up about it, but in times like these, when a small child was shaking and shaking, it would be better to be safe than sorry. *Stay with the plan.*

The hospital driveway was empty, the light that belched from the lobby blinding them momentarily. Bright but unmanned, the lobby posed no obstacle, not even the need to explain to a person where they wanted to go. They already knew where Emergency was and needed no guidance.

'Our daughter's shivering, with a high fever. Can we please admit her?' Tarisa asked the staff at the registration desk. She saw Mia shuffling on Chris' shoulder, her eyes slowly opening and registering the room bleached whiter than an eggshell. It was becoming clearer and clearer that the shivering would not return. It was something that Mia's body had needed to do once and get over with.

So now that they were here, the agenda changed. Tarisa wanted Mia to be fine, and fine *in here*. She remembered her washer-dryer still spinning at home. The vomit, the middle-of-the-night showering—these were not things she wanted to repeat. Looking at the waiting room's faraway walls and deep hallways, she wanted herself to be able to rest in this space. It was as if she had been swallowed into the intestines of respite. *Go farther and farther in, away from the space that is home.*

'You'll have to see the doctor first,' the receptionist answered, looking up from her computer screen for the first time. She slapped the registration form and a pen on the counter, which Tarisa thought was impolite, but she didn't really mind, as long as she could have the stay. She knew that the chances of any doctor declining to admit Mia would be slim. There was no reason for doctors to say no to money unless they were good people who suspected that the families of patients would be troubled by the spending. A doctor here couldn't be that kind of person if they were working at a private hospital known to charge exorbitant fees, and Tarisa and Chris couldn't be completely troubled by spending since they had chosen to come here.

When they finally met a doctor ten minutes later, he said, 'Admitting? Sure, if that would make you comfortable.' There was no protest. In fact, he seemed to jump at their offer. The gladness that he tried to subdue flashed in a brief smile. 'A paediatrician will come and check on your daughter in the morning then,' he said.

'Tomorrow's Saturday. I'll apply for childcare leave for today,' Chris said when they were alone again. He applied for childcare leave on his phone while they waited for the nurse to complete the paperwork that would transfer them to the children's ward. Chris' quota for childcare leave was two days per year, an amount so little that Tarisa felt it was sarcastic, a subtle dig at men who cared about their offspring.

'Please follow me,' a new nurse said. They stood and she turned, walking with her clipboard to the elevator. She did not look back or make conversation, and this made Tarisa want the stay more.

Mia was flopped over Chris' shoulder. Tarisa was holding onto bags. They walked past paintings of flowers and lakes. Nobody else was in the hallway. Tarisa made a note to herself that if she ever needed to come to the hospital again, she should come around this time, before 6 a.m., when it is serene and the wait short.

The elevator doors sliced open on the eighth floor. 'This way, please,' the nurse said and gestured to the right. Of course, she didn't know that they had been here before, that they knew the ward like they knew Mia's school. The first time Mia was hospitalized, after Shanghai, Tarisa had been truly frightened. This time, she was calmly looking forward to rest.

Past a small garden, the nurse pressed a buzzer in front of glass double-doors. They inhaled the family into a cove, disconnected from any outpatients. The children's ward was colourful, artificial, and sterile, just the way Tarisa remembered it to be. There was no noise typically associated with hospitals—no beat from any machine, no PA announcements. The only thing reminding Tarisa that this was a hospital were visual clues: a Stryker bed on standby, cartoon stickers lining the walls, the nurses' station at the end. Tarisa began to feel a warm calm soothing her from top to bottom.

'It's her,' Chris said. Tarisa turned around to see who he was talking about. 'Look at her legs. It's the one with the very dry skin.' The nurse who had brought them here handed her clipboard to this new person and disappeared dutifully. Tarisa watched her slipping through the double-doors, moving on with her day, like the ships near the port that had gone on earlier in the night.

Tarisa turned back. *Geetha.* she remembered the woman's name now. Indeed, they had met her last year. Memories returned bit by bit. Geetha, whose dry skin Chris remembered—because, well, what else does one have to pay attention to when enclosed in a ward for three days?— seemed the same. She left her young face bare, showing the olive of her skin. Her face's only ornamentation were eyeglasses—simple, frameless, accenting just how raw she allowed herself to appear to the world.

From the way her eyes didn't linger on them with recognition, Tarisa could tell Geetha did not remember them.

She brought them into a room in front of the nurses' station, which Tarisa realized wasn't ideal. The nurses liked to chat, especially if somebody was just coming into a shift. She considered asking for a room change but realized that it would mean more paperwork, which meant delaying their settling in. Chris must now want to go back to sleep. Mia, too, should get more rest.

The asymmetrical layout of the room jumped out to her. Its sharp edges sliced into Tarisa's attention and made her feel more alert.

The room was ready to serve every basic need of comfort: a bathroom to the right, a writing desk at the end of the hallway, a sofa bed next to it, a large window settled into half the wall. In front of the sofa bed was a cot. Between the cot and the bathroom was a wardrobe. On the other side of the cot, next to the sofa bed: a side table and a dressing table. A television was mounted high on the wall, so that the child in the cot could get a good view.

Geetha lowered the rail, and Chris put Mia in the cot. She sat with her back straight and scanned the room. Her lips began to quiver, and wrinkles slowly rippled in between her eyebrows. Mia also remembered this place and what had happened in it. It was largely a different memory from her mother's.

Geetha did not address Mia. She turned to Tarisa and Chris and began to point out where the linens were for the sofa bed. 'Don't worry about it. We've been here before. In fact, I think we were with you,' Tarisa said.

Geetha's smile widened. 'You looked familiar when you came in,' she said. Although Tarisa hadn't spotted signs of her recognition and didn't know if Geetha was only trying to be polite, she realized that it didn't matter. She planted her weekend bag on the side table and could almost hear the contents and their eagerness of waiting to come out.

CHAPTER 9

From that October onwards, after he had told her that her ambition was useless, Tarisa had become quieter around Chris. Sometimes, she felt like she was lurking underneath her own skin.

She thought about unpacking. She thought about a life that wouldn't have existed here at all. Their things should be in America. He had said several times that Boston was unnecessary, but maybe she could still make a case.

From Chris' point of view, ambition didn't make sense when money was abundant. She could see that from a practical perspective. She had been experiencing much more comfort ever since they had become a couple: Amtrak trains could be taken instead of buses (Chris wanted to pay for it), cabs could be taken instead of subway trains (Chris wanted to pay for it), teeth could be straightened with Invisalign instead of wiry braces (Chris' insurance policy, once again). They had holidayed in Europe, driving around, waking up in hotels, not hostels. Not to mention that they always ate wherever they wanted to eat—which, in this case, was whatever Chris wanted to eat, because she never proposed what she couldn't pay for. The lifestyle that came with being his partner was already more than sufficient. What was she really when she said she wanted more? Was it greed?

She never knew how much of her family's Buddhist values made her wince thinking about this word. Greed was a vice, and a foolish one of chasing after illusions. But maybe it wasn't even Buddhism that spoke to her. Maybe it was just knowing that so much of the world lived with more difficulty, significantly. She had once googled their income to see their income ranking. With Chris' income alone, they were already among the world's top 10 per cent. What would her ambition, or greed, be for? She could not answer that question.

She began to slow her thoughts down.

What, really, is a life that doesn't question what's enough?

The ambition that she had was a difficult kind, unrelated to practicality, and he could be moved only by practicality. She, too, was starting to question whether she should, whether giving in wouldn't, in fact, be the sensible thing to do.

Their conversations usually turned into the same argument, where she would listen to how he was so convinced that they had enough. She would continue to ask to go back to Boston, even though she had begun to wonder more and more, each time, whether she should just settle for a life that was 'enough' here.

As if bonding with his mind, she would perceive him for the obstacle that he was, but also contemplate his values, even trying to identify in it a truth that she— younger, less financially successful, generally more disorderly—could learn.

He was never satisfied when she said that she had a drive, a rarely felt drive, to embark on and complete this PhD, even when she tried to use this as a point of discussion, not argument. It seemed he had done some homework too, since he countered with well-padded responses. 'This doesn't *have* to be what you do. You're good at many things,' he would say, or some variation of the thought.

But one day, he hit home too hard. 'PhD research is different. It's not the fun stuff you do in your master's.' She heard it—the unexpected condescension, an overstep that showed underestimation and disrespect for her mind.

'Julia said she wanted me *because* I took a PhD *research class*,' she said, looking him in the eye.

'Working alone when coursework is done is different.'

What did he think she went to school for? Fun?

She saw the trap that she had caught herself in by marrying a man who was older and had already gone through the experience that she wanted for herself. She had met him when he was already a 'doctor'. He could always give her his version of how a PhD lifestyle would be. He could make her current desire something he'd advise against in hindsight. Just as she was beginning to realize this, he said, 'The job market for academia is really tough. It's not like you go into a PhD and you're guaranteed a job. If you're lucky, you might get a job in, I don't know, Kansas or Kentucky.'

Kansas or Kentucky? Who cares whether it was Kansas or Kentucky? Throughout life, she had been tugged along with suitcases to places whose names didn't matter. Home was anywhere a suitcase got unpacked, and no place ever held a suitcase shut. 'What's wrong with Kansas or Kentucky?'

'There's nothing there.'

'There is.' She could see the campuses clearly in her head: quadrangles, large buildings, pedestrians on tree-lined walkways. 'There are universities.'

'And what about my job?'

'You fell in love with me when I was going into a PhD in Comp Lit. *That* was also Kansas or Kentucky. Why? What's with it now?'

'I don't know, T.'

'Why are you caring about it *now*?'

'I said I don't know.'

'I'd be coming from Harvard. It's probably not going to be Kansas or Kentucky,' she said but wasn't completely convinced herself. Chris' Yale degree hadn't brought him an academic position at a top-tier institution. He had told her he had interviewed at only 'second-rate institutions'. But she remembered why this had happened: He hadn't even wanted to try being in academia; the road was too strenuous. He knew he could be in Washington and make good money, working nowhere near as hard as classmates vying to be professors.

I do want to become a professor, and it is natural for me to work hard. I am his classmates, who got to the top. I am not him.

'Is a PhD in education actually better?' he asked.

'Better than what?'

'I meant are the prospects of getting a job actually decent?'

He seemed genuinely curious, and she wondered if he wasn't sliding her a chance. His openness made her also want to be decent. She didn't know the answer to his question, and now that she felt they were angling towards reason and reality, she changed her tone to be more inquisitive, too. 'I don't know. Is it?' *If it were, would he reconsider?* 'Should we, I don't know, find out?'

She seemed to have reminded him that perhaps in a marriage, there was supposed to be compromise, and perhaps decisions should be made based on the reasonableness of a situation, not personal desires.

'You want me to, like, google it?'

He nodded.

'Now?'

'Yeah.' His nods quickened, and she could see genuine allyship bob up and down. There was nothing threatening in the way he seemed to signal agreeability. She was surprised that the conversation had come to this, but, again, she had not married a monster. He had just displayed a moment of extreme bizarreness, for some reason, and she could let it slip.

She reached for her computer on the dining table, flooded with books they had both borrowed from the library—fiction for her, non-fiction for him.

'Am I getting the search words right?' she asked after she found no useful information. 'Can you think of anything else?'

He shook his head. 'Not really.'

'Fuck.'

An unhelpful search would return them to a stalemate, where she was likely to lose. There were bags she could just pack and leave with, but whenever she imagined rolling them towards their apartment door, she also saw his sad face, his lack of support and enthusiasm for what she wanted to be off to pursue. She had come too far in the marriage for bags to be the only thing she could consider.

She knew that he could be right about the job market being harsh. Maybe he was wrong. Maybe he was right. Why did it matter, though? Before he had come along, difficulty factored little in her decision-making. As long as she was not being asked to do the hard science of proofs in mathematics, research did not scare her. The harder a social science topic was to understand, the more books she could acquire, the deeper she learned about something. The harder something was to synthesize, the more she could think and increase the chances of coming up with original ideas.

'We stay. I mean, we don't *need* to go. We have everything here. Jobs. Money,' he restarted.

She said nothing. What was there to add?

He became comfortable in the silence that she made room for, deleting herself. In it, he found momentum. 'Here, our parents are close by. It takes me two hours to fly to Bangkok.'

Her eyes lifted to him. 'Parents?' She knew that Chris was constantly worried about his. '*Parents?* Is that what this is actually about? Being close to your mother and father?' His parents were septuagenarians, and his mother was particularly lonely. His father had been emotionally absent ever since a debilitating car accident before Chris' birth. The old man had a memory that couldn't expand, and therefore no new desire or habits groomed since the seventies. He only kept repeating his lifestyle from before the accident, when he was a doctoral student at Princeton (Chris, she sometimes realized, unimpressed, was as intelligent as he was partially because of genetics). He clipped newspapers in the attic all day long, collecting data for papers he handwrote, which no publishers would take.

Your parents? she wanted to say. *What's there to like about your parents? Your father hoards newspapers. Your mother shops all day long. Their home is disgusting, filled with newspaper and clothes no one needs.*

'No, it's not just parents. I mean, it's, it's everything!'

'What is "everything"?'

He was confusing her. For once, this confusion seemed unplanned. Chris looked like a kid cracking under pressure. His mouth moved like it was trying to hold in the words. 'It's everything!'

She wanted to pull the words off his tongue. 'What, Chris?'

'Everything.'

'What? I liked our everything! What was *your* everything?'

'Life in America,' he said.

'*What* life in America?'

'Life in America! I mean, it's not so easy being—'

She couldn't imagine what it would be that he could want to run away from this much. He loved the barbecues (which meant Kansas and Kentucky should have been fine), the jazz scene, the easiness of his job. Confusion, she knew, was a labyrinth of uncomfortable truths. The conversation was starting to be real.

'You're not going to understand this,' he said.

'I haven't understood much anyway.'

'It's difficult to be an Asian man there.'

He explained it to her in a way she wasn't sure how to refute. She listened doubtfully but intently, the way a child might listen to a parable, feeling removed yet eager to spot the relevance to their own lives.

He said that he had been feeling, the entire time in America, like he was at the bottom rung of society.

'I don't fucking get it,' she quipped. 'You're from Yale, and you work in DC.'

'As a man,' he said.

'A man what?' she cut him off, impatient. The energy from being dragged into a series of reasons, unconnected, one after the other, was starting to decrease the sense of time she felt she had for him.

'I'm nothing.'

'How is Doctor-Chris-from-Yale-who-works-in-DC-and-makes-so-much-money nothing? We've been spending our weekends unpacking boxes borne out of your success.' She gestured to the piano. 'A whole grand Steinway.'

'Because as a man, I am nothing.'

She raised her palms incredulously. 'What the fuck, Chris? You're married to me. Why would we be married if I thought you were nothing?'

'Can you please stop saying *fuck*?'

She did not answer him.

'You don't understand.'

'Well, help me,' she tried to stop herself but could manage only saying it more softly, 'fucking understand.'

It was clear that he had never articulated this. The squirmy curves his face began to pick up, the sense of agitation she saw in his lips, which began to rotate between mild quivers and pursing, showed that he was running into an emotional breakthrough, which she could only hope would yield the real, final answer.

'White men are on top, and then there are the Black guys, and then there's, you know,' he said in a small voice, 'Asian men.'

'What about Latino men?'

'They're still above us.'

'Says who?'

'It's in the culture, in the society.'

'Chris, you're married to *me*.' She wanted to hint that maybe he was doing just all right.

'My attractiveness is below my black security guard's. And I don't mean to be mean or say something is wrong with being a security guard. That's not the point. The point is: in America, I'm—' he seemed to have difficulty finding the word. His brows furrowed. 'Like. . .' he repeated, over and over.

'Like what?' She waited this time, for his 'likes' to sound completed, before interrupting him.

'You don't understand. It doesn't matter. As a man, I'm at the bottom. It's this general feeling that they view me as weak.'

'Asian men are emasculated. That's your woe?'

They were not going back to the US because living in his body was tough, and not practical-tough, not ambitious-tough, but physically, it was a trap. He could work on getting his money, she could work on lowering her ambitions, but no one would be able to leave their body. She saw it now: she couldn't win.

She had never thought that masculinity was so important to him, a man who was typically more gentle than alpha, but she sensed that the emasculation of Asian men in the US was real, and the thing he was trying to run away from. She found herself thinking about her tightknit group of six Asian American girlfriends: five of them dated white men, whom they would all later marry this year. Then, beyond that tight-knit group, there were a few couples she had noticed in Boston and DC, where the women were Asian and the men white; there was no one she knew who was an Asian man with a white woman besides one couple, *yes, that one couple*, she tried to be fair; then, there were the mothers whom she knew here: if they were Asian, they were either married to an Asian man or a white man, but if they were white women, they were never married to an Asian man—*no, there was that one couple, too.* Then, of course, if she just thought about Thailand, it didn't take much to realize the numerous couplings of white men with Thai women who openly declared their love for *farang—but that, of course, was often a financial relationship, the New York Times had even run an article about it a few years ago.*

She thought about her Asian American girl friends at Harvard, intelligent and proud women who wouldn't marry for anything less than love.

It's—what is it—probably something related to his emasculation. Their emasculation. The emasculation of Asian men. Most people seem to not want to talk about this. He's not American, but he was there, breathing it in daily.

She would later pose her questions to the internet because it was too awkward, and possibly damaging, to ask her own friends how they would explain why all their partners were white men.

They would get defensive, even if I went up to them with open arms, saying, 'Educate me. Please, tell me. It might be related to why my husband self-ejected from your country, the reason I am now here permanently. Remember: I speak American English, but I'm not American.'

She saw Chris as she had never seen him—a man actually worried about something, and not about something practical, but existential. She had always thought he breezed through life, indifferent, almost un-self-aware.

'Well, I guess I can't change the fact that you'll always be an Asian man,' she said, sounding more callous than how she felt inside. Her opposition ended here, not because she felt it as the end internally, but because she had learned, from absorbing progressive America, to silence herself for those who claimed being victimized by oppression. It would take months, maybe years, to really let any of this seep in before she could say, 'Yes! Yes, that emasculation! Let it drive us out of the US!' But if she wanted to start doing the right thing, she would have to begin now, and that was by letting him stay here and herself, passage into the vision he had of a life less shattering.

One day after another, she stayed in her kidnapped life, quashing her own career path little by little. Each time ambition pollinated in her head, she squeezed her eyes shut until she aborted the little dreams it wanted to fertilize. She told herself that she was doing the right thing. She was protecting her husband from the emasculation he so feared in the US—assuming it was truly the problem.

Assuming it was truly the problem was the only thing she could do. It was a weighty, unfalsifiable claim.

CHAPTER 10

'I'll take the cot,' Tarisa said to Chris. 'Mia, sweetheart, let's change your clothes.' Tarisa began to undress her.

'Why I need to change?' Mia asked, her eyes now fully open.

'You're a patient,' Tarisa replied. 'You have a uniform. Like at school.'

Mia found that funny. She began to laugh.

They left Mia on the bed, taking turns to answer her questions.

'Why are we here?'

'Because you're sick,' Tarisa said.

'Will we go home tomorrow?'

'Probably not,' Chris said.

'Will the nurses give me ouchie?'

'A very small ouchie,' Tarisa said and hung their clothes in the wardrobe. She saw a pair of adult slippers and the deposit safe inside. She couldn't imagine using it; either she or Chris would be in this room with Mia anyway. She wished there were two pairs of slippers. The meals, too, were set up for the child and only one adult.

Only one parent is expected to stay. In our family, it's two.

Tarisa flicked a light switch in front of the bathroom and walked inside. She saw a familiar woman in the mirror: one whose internal world took up more space than anyone around her ever knew. Outwardly, the woman was small: with breasts leftover from the drainage of milk, and eyes that held a history of remove. Her irises held back. She was familiar with distance and distance-keeping. Around her, small cornflower blue tiles crept up.

She placed her toothbrush and Mia's by the sink next to each other and let out a sigh, exiting the bathroom she thought possessed an overtone of a pool where air was water.

Full-time parenting was more tiring than anything she had ever known. Every older woman—fellow mothers, Mia's teachers, her own mother, and Chris' mother—had told her that Mia was an easy child, but Tarisa still felt sorrow pushing into spaces that made up who she was inside. She could understand what those women meant. She had seen rowdy children, their mothers sitting behind, looking frail and out of breath. She knew that those were the kids who were 'difficult', making their mothers sick (but sometimes they seemed energized by that sickness, sometimes they had the energy to scream, to vent, to clean messes and be pregnant with the third or fourth child). Mia, au contraire, was easy. A child like her should uplift.

Tarisa tapped her phone to see the time, but instead saw messages from Regina to a small group: breakfast the following week—will it or will it not happen; and if it will happen, where and what time? Another Facebook message from another friend, asking if she'd be in Bangkok soon. (Tarisa did not like this one. She had used Tarisa for free labour last time.)

She looked at Regina's suggestions: a café on Orchard Road. Apparently, it had fantastic blueberry French toast, soaked overnight, topped with caramelized banana, hazelnut praline fudge, and coffee foam. As Tarisa imagined the things they would talk about—children, because that's the only thing Regina ever wanted to talk about—she also realized that she could eat a cold, hard piece of bread, and she would not care.

One of the things that Chris despised the most about the hospital stay was that the nurses would frequently come to measure Mia's vital signs. Tarisa knew how much he hated their interruptions, but his discomfort didn't stop Tarisa from hoping to spend at least two nights here. She crawled onto the cot with Mia as Chris dimmed the lights. It was her second time going to bed in twelve hours without kissing him. Lately, she hadn't been finding him attractive. Sometimes, she even felt repelled.

Through the cot railings, Tarisa watched Chris insert his earplugs and slide the hospital's waffle blanket over his body. Its swaddle-like texture matched the infantility that she was coming to associate with him, even though she knew that manliness was not the product of only lust, but also an ability to love deeply, the way Chris had been showing he did through acts of service, especially after Mia's birth.

She heard him turn on the sofa's faux leather, making a squishy sound as he tried to find his comfort.

In the cot, Tarisa' legs curled so that she could fit. Underneath her nose, Mia's head waited, like a giant cabbage. She sniffed Mia's scalp and hair, which no longer oozed the milky newborn scent that Chris had preserved by keeping her first set of clothing in a Ziploc bag (where he had kept his tadalafil—it was what helped to make Mia then, but it had no effect now).

Tarisa exhaled and began syncing her breath with Mia's, which she could make out by placing her hand on her swelling and flattening belly. She watched Mia's body respond to her exhales, melting down into the cot each time. Air-conditioning on the scalp seemed a little cruel for a child.

She unlocked her phone and sighed as she typed, 'Yes, breakfast,' with a smile emoji to Regina. Tarisa liked her but did not enjoy her company. Regina steered conversations to talk only about their children's schedules: music and dance classes. Sometimes even competitive chess. The get-togethers always turned into a bleeding directory of the 'best teachers' for 'enrichment' opportunities. Tarisa had nothing to contribute. Mia went to swimming classes—this was how she had met Regina—and nothing more. The swimming teacher Mia had wasn't the best, but Mia's life never seemed at risk in his hands. She estimated that Regina spent about 1 per cent of their time talking about non-motherhood and imagined that that was how this woman, in fact, experienced life and her body: a state of maternal flow.

Tarisa wanted to get to know more people, especially the parents from school, in case anyone shared her temperament and could hold an interesting conversation, but they were mostly Western Europeans possessing a culture Tarisa had not yet learned to navigate. Their slower, less rowdy camaraderie, where newcomers didn't jut out hands round-the-clock for self-introductions and conversations were kept brief, soft, and polite, hampered her seeing a place for herself. She derived no happiness from small talk. For now, Regina was all she had.

A phone rang at the nurse's station, reminding Tarisa that sleep would not be smooth in the ward, but that was a price still worth paying. She didn't need much sleep if the nurses would be around. Chris did not seem as resigned. He still fought the noise, drawing the waffle blanket over his whole head now. Luckily for her, he didn't play blame games. He wouldn't fault her that they were here, ruining his sleep, though to her, how she had manipulated the circumstances were clear.

By now, Chris was both her friend and her enemy. She kept a part of him close and another part closer. She was careful in what she said to him, knowing that he wouldn't strive for anything that seemed unnecessary, and that what he deemed necessary—being an Asian man in Asia—was not his need that she could, or should, refute. She no longer took him for an unconditional supporter and knew that if she had any dreams for herself, she might have to walk that path on her own. After all, he was a man, socialized into assuming his own interests were less flexible and more important, especially if he could provide the money to cover basic needs. She still loved him, but now with both eyes open.

Tarisa speculated that he had really meant no conscious harm that October. He sincerely could not understand the purpose of ambition when they already had what they did. What he needed—he laid it out in fewer than five fingers after she had asked, 'You really don't want a promotion?'—was 'a family that I can support, jazz, and time to read.' Here was the family he was supporting. At home was the piano where he played his jazz. Whenever he was not attending to the family or the piano, was time to read.

CHAPTER 11

'Blood pressure and temperature.' Geetha lowered the rail, while an older nurse, who also looked familiar, handed her a thermometer. There was no evidence that time had passed. The room was still marked by familiar shadows and filtered light.

Mia's body wriggled when the thermometer crept into her ear. She tried to toss to turn it out, but when Geetha reinserted it, more firmly this time, she cried before she even sat up.

'Mommy, can you hold Mia down?'

Tarisa cooperated, placing her hand on Mia's buttocks, not pinning her down, but hoping to calm her.

'Mommy!' Mia began to say.

'Mia, it's just temperature and blood pressure,' Tarisa said. Mia turned and gripped Tarisa's fingers tightly. Her legs began to kick when the older nurse—*G-something*—tried to put the blood pressure reader on her big toe. 'Don't kick, sweetie. The nurses can't read your blood pressure if you kick.' Tarisa stretched out an arm to hold Mia's legs down, while keeping a hand available for her grip.

G-something read out a number for the blood pressure, which Tarisa didn't understand. 'Thirty-eight point five,' Geetha said, pulling out the thermometer.

'My name is Nurse Gracie,' the older nurse said to Tarisa, smiling, introducing herself with a hand on her chest after all the tools had been pushed aside. 'Mia, how are you feeling?'

Mia began to cry.

'Okay, never mind, dear. Maybe later, after you get some rest. Bye-bye, dear.' Gracie cocked her head and widened her eyes at Mia. Tarisa thought of her own mother. They must be around the same age, in their late fifties. Both were confident with children.

'Doctor Dhivya will be with you shortly, at about eight o'clock,' Gracie said. That was only two hours away.

'Thank you.' She watched as Geetha rolled their equipment out.

As soon as the nurses disappeared, Tarisa turned to Chris. He had not yet come out of his slumber or removed his earplugs or eye mask. The nurses' arrival had caused a commotion. He could not have been soundly asleep. He wouldn't have been so disengaged if they were home alone, but now that they were here, he must be thinking that his wife could handle the situation, since there were the nurses here to help. *He's not wrong.*

When Tarisa opened her eyes again, it was morning. She held it in her eyes.

Tarisa recognized the body standing beside her bed. Tall, towering, pudgy. She assessed the doctor slowly from bottom to top, noting the black slacks, paisley tunic, and frizzy curls. *Not Barbie.* She wasn't sure which she said first, 'Good morning' or, 'I'm sorry,' but the doctor said, 'It's okay.'

Doctor Dhivya's word came through her smile. 'We'll be taking her blood sample,' she said, looking into Tarisa's eyes, making a connection. Mia was still asleep. Tarisa turned to see if Chris was awake and listening. He was still cocooned, facing the wall.

It's still my turn, and that's okay. He's never been excited about meeting new people anyway.

She looked at the clock. It was just after 8 a.m.

'Mia's going to cry a lot when she finds out,' Tarisa said.

'Well, it will need to be done,' Doctor Dhivya said as a matter of fact, which Tarisa could understand.

'Should I wake her up?'

'Yes, please.'

Tarisa tapped Mia's shoulder. 'Mia, sweetheart. Wake up, sweetie, the doctor needs to check you.' Mia began to cough a little.

'I hear the cough,' the doctor said.

'Yes, the very real cough,' Tarisa said.

Waking from her stupor, Mia was unhappy.

Tarisa gave her shoulder a push. She was surprised to find her daughter so heavy. When had Mia become so big? *Did I not know because Chris was usually the one manually handling her, into the shower, onto the bed, off the bed?* The doctor walked closer towards Mia, touched her chest, and placed the stethoscope to listen to the sounds inside.

'Just a little bit, Mia. Let's get this done quickly, sweetie,' Tarisa said. Mia's face scrunched up and surprised her mother when she didn't cry.

'Mia, can you breathe in?' the doctor asked. Tarisa inhaled to show Mia what the doctor meant. Mia resisted. She tried to peel Tarisa's fingers off her body.

'Mia, sweetie, just a few times, and then we'll be done. Come on, just breathe in.'

Mia began to inhale, her body extending like a rehydrated raisin.

Good, good child.

'Breathe out. Good, Mia. Now, can you just open your mouth for me and say, "Ah"?'

Mia shook her head.

'Just a little bit, Mia. Let's get this done quickly, sweetie,' Tarisa said.

Mia opened her mouth but didn't say 'ah'. The doctor tried to put a spatula on her tongue, but Mia pulled her face away.

'It's okay. I saw her throat. She's got some inflammation,' the doctor said. 'Let me check her temperature now.' The doctor inserted a thermometer into Mia's ears. Tarisa held Mia's head still, putting slight pressure on either temple. 'Thirty-eight point seven. That's pretty high. I'll give her medicine for her fever and some antibiotics. Then we'll monitor her. If she responds to the antibiotics, that will mean it's likely just a bacterial infection that we can get rid of.'

Tarisa liked that diagnosis. It sounded benign. 'So, what are we looking at? Two nights here?'

'We'll see from the blood test.'

'Is it anything serious?'

'We'll have to wait for the blood test to know, but it's likely a bacterial or viral infection.'

'Medicine, Mommy?' Mia said. 'But I don't want medicine.'

Chris began to shift under the blanket.

'Just a little bit of medicine,' the doctor said.

'It'll taste like orange or strawberry,' Tarisa said.

'Yes, it's orange-flavoured. You like oranges, Mia?' the doctor said.

'I don't like medicine,' Mia said.

'Yes, she likes oranges,' Tarisa said.

Tarisa took a snapshot of Mia and sent it to Leela. 'In the hospital for a fever. Nothing serious. Just better safe than sorry!' she captioned. She planned to send this photo so that Leela wouldn't find out about the hospital stay by accident—which is to say by calling and catching them there. It would only make her more worried, for she would think that Mia's condition was so severe that they weren't able to even find time to let her know. She would then get anxious and call or text them frequently to ask for updates. Tarisa wanted her hospital stay to be calmer than that, so she sent a shot of Mia staring off somewhere while sitting up and looking strong.

The photo captured the serenity of being here. If they were at home, Tarisa would be screaming at Mia while trying to get her to take her medicine. Mia would be crying and pushing the medicine away from Tarisa's hands.

Tarisa thought that she had tried everything. She would always start off calmly, talking about the need for medicine and sharing anecdotes of sweet, delicious syrups when she was a child. Mia would seem to give in, but then she would quickly pull away as soon as the spoon would touch her lips. Then, once the convincing worked and Mia finally swallowed the medicine, she would spit it all back out. No amount of juice chasers helped. The whole ordeal could take up to two hours. Even Leela, whose visit once coincided with Mia's illness, gave up, stomping off and handing Tarisa the spoon.

Nurse Gracie, a petite woman with the grip of a boa constrictor, could hold Mia down and inject medicine into her throat with a syringe. Tarisa had thought herself capable of similar ruthlessness until last year, when she saw Chris try to perform Nurse Gracie's manoeuvre at home. She had yelled, 'Chris! Stop! It looks so cruel! Don't do that to our child!' He stepped back and began to apologize, confused, 'Oh, I'm sorry. I'm sorry. I thought it's what you wanted. How would you like me to do it?' She realized that what she had wanted was patience. She took the spoon from his hand, balancing the medicine. An hour or two later, all of it was in Mia's body. She got up from the floor, where she had crouched to be eye-to-eye with Mia, and cleaned the spoon in the sink, leaving it on the rack to use again four hours later. As for why she had this patience when it seemed she would be the last person in the world to do so, she wasn't sure. She could only think that it was because she needed to have it—no one else would.

Tarisa let Chris wake up at his own time. Surely, he had heard Doctor Dhivya in the room and had just chosen to ignore her. This phrase, 'chosen to ignore', was perhaps too judgmental—he was sleepy and had given his energy to scrubbing a soiled toddler just hours earlier; he'd even volunteered to brush her teeth; he had been giving all of himself. Tarisa didn't want to wake him up, not now, on the first morning, risking setting the wrong tone. He should feel that this ward demanded no more than his regular contributions.

It was close to nine o'clock when he removed his eye mask and pulled out his earplugs. Tarisa was satisfied seeing this. She had observed that if he started his day with them at nine o'clock, he lasted longer as a parent, he lasted longer as someone wanting to contribute.

If today were a regular Friday, Tarisa would have found herself with a three-hour window to be alone, and then she'd be with Mia after preschool before Chris got home. She and Mia would have lunch together. There would be rice and crumbs spilled all over the floor, and Mia would get dirty and need a shower after the meal. Mia might do many things that would make Tarisa walk around the apartment non-stop, cleaning this, tidying up that. Mia might challenge anything she said ('No!' 'I don't want to!' 'Why!'). Tarisa would explain until she ran out of energy, and when Mia still prompted her, 'Why, Mom?' she might snap, feeling her neck rip off her shoulders, negativity erupting, spraying all over Mia, whom she would later have to wash with warm, soothing words and caressing reminders of love.

I'm sorry, that was just a moment, a moment that I shouldn't have had. I was tired. I'm sorry, I'm sorry.

Here, at the hospital, sure, they were together all the time, but Mia was—Tarisa could think of no other word for it—*disempowered*. How odd, that seeing Mia in a cot, looking confined, she wanted to ask her to keep being disempowered: *Please, only for two days. I could live here, slowing down, instead of thinking about all the housework and how to entertain you before your father gets home.*

Here, time felt like it followed no hands. A specific time was not a thing she had to chase. Time was in the background, like air. She imagined how the rest of the day would unfold, with Mia in the crib for most of it. They would still spend a lot of time in the same room, but there were so many more people who could come in and take care of things. She did not have to wait for Chris, for five o'clock and ten minutes. Nurse Gracie could help with the medicine. Geetha or housekeeping could change bedsheets if there was a leaky diaper. There would be no toys, so Tarisa wouldn't be asked to play.

And you will be woken up often enough for temperature checks and medicine that you will be too tired to play, so you will just stare at the walls and daydream.

If she could make Chris feel happy in this place, Tarisa wouldn't need to hide that she herself was happy here.

She felt her skin release its tight hook on her bones as she envisioned them all boxed off in this room, enjoying a simpler life for a few days. She wished Chris would also be able to see it as a vacation, that he wouldn't, as he typically would, view wakeful rest as boredom. She would have to work on him, too, if he found this ward boring. She wanted to rest simply, with everyone on the same page.

He looked confused as he rose.

'Good morning,' she said. 'How'd you sleep?'

'Okay. Still a bit tired.'

'Of course. Feel free to go back to sleep if you need some more rest.'

She never said such things at home. In the mornings, she'd wait for his eyes to flicker open and immediately ask Mia to go and be with him, so that she could clean the apartment or continue scrolling through job portals. She had started and quit three jobs since their arrival in Singapore. First, she had a food writing job, the one that was meant for a gap year. Four months in, she quit that, along with three others in the five-person office; the boss was getting too rude, he cursed them out every day—too often for a life that she now understood would be in Singapore indefinitely. (The only person who stayed on was the accountant, his wife. *Wives, they stay.*) Soon after, Tarisa waited tables at a friend's café, waiting for other potential employers to give her something better to do. (Nothing: no one ever got back to her, even if she had embellished her resumé to the best of her abilities, with Chris helping her out. They both knew that they had to work extra hard for companies to be able to justify to the government that they needed to hire her over Singaporean citizens, if the position was at all even open to foreigners.) Then, there was the third job: the ideal one, until a Mr Ooi became the boss, and she would hear the harshest words ever said to the mother in her.

Chris sat up, blinking, then blew out a sigh and stood to pick up his phone. 'All's good. Boss says, "No problem about leave".' He held up a finger in the air. 'One sec. Just saw another email.' He hummed reading it. Then, the hum suddenly stopped. He woke fully. 'You won't believe this, T! The office just hired a new copy editor and they're paying him two hundred dollars per hour!' For years, Chris had been playing the unofficial copy editor for the whole office on top of his actual role.

'Why? Were you not doing a good job?' she teased.

'Don't know, T! Maybe I wasn't.'

'Bullshit,' she said right away. 'But it *is* bullshit, right? They'll pay someone for the task only if they're not already on payroll.'

'Yeah.'

'I guess they just needed someone official.'

'Or maybe corruption.'

'Probably corruption. In which case,' she said after a brief pause, 'your office should get me to do it.' 'We could split the money,' she quickly added when he didn't respond. She didn't know where that remark had come from. Chris still never talked about needing or wanting more.

'You *could* do it.'

She wondered if it was the remark about splitting that had encouraged him. They had never talked about having a more business-like marriage, but since the passion was dead, she wondered if this wouldn't be a route to take more transparently. 'I could. But I also can't, right?'

'Right.'

'Because I'm your wife. Your office isn't *that* corrupt,' she said, almost as a question. She knew that if she weren't his wife, there would be a chance that she could market herself as a copy editor and do it. She was obsessed about perfecting every written thing.

'Right.' He put his phone back into his bag, then rummaged around.

She looked at his buttocks, hidden behind thick sweatpants. He never wore these at home. She saw these sweatpants only when they holidayed. She hoped he was already associating this hospital with leisure.

'I forgot to bring my supplements,' he sighed.

At home, it was his routine to wake up every morning and take his supplements right away. They were supposed to help him return to a healthier hormone level, but since they hadn't had sex since Mia's conception, Tarisa wanted to tell him, 'Forget about the supplements. They don't make a difference. Stay here with us.'

'Are you going to go home and get them?' she asked, knowing the answer.

'Yeah. Do you want me to get you anything from home?'

'I'll write you a list.' Tarisa took a notepad and pen from the desk and began to write down what she saw she could now also have: vitamin C serum, hyaluronic acid and, when she remembered she'd be going out tonight, mascara, eyeshadow, and eyeliner. 'I have Edwina's workshop this evening, and then the show tonight, but I don't need to go if you want me to stay.'

'No, no, don't be silly! You should go!' Chris said. She always wondered if his enthusiasm about her dancing would be there if he had never betrayed her. Was he compensating for how he had stopped her from pursuing that most-wanted PhD years ago? Maybe he thought she could find little pleasures now, and they would add up to something as meaningful. She could never feel completely grateful for his enthusiasm, even if she had heard other mothers describe their situations, the opposite: no hobbies because their husbands wouldn't be home to watch the children, and they all accepted this as the status quo. Chris was always with Mia whenever she wanted to dance or go to a show.

'Thanks.' She handed him the list. 'Oh, and if it's not too much, my laptop too?' She needed to proofread a friend's piece of fiction. She thought about the copy editor Chris' office was about to pay two hundred dollars an hour to and how she was about to proofread her friend's writing for free.

'Sure.' He swung his backpack on his shoulder and put his wallet in his pocket. It was always the last step before he left a room. 'I'm gonna go get the stuff. I'll be back in an hour or so.'

'Take your time.' She followed him to the door. She pecked him, squeezed his torso, and looked into his eyes. 'Cross the road safely.'

'Bye, Daddy!' Mia shouted from the cot. She had been quiet all along, gifting her parents unknowingly. Tarisa looked at Mia, then at the mounted television. Her silence had been freeing, space Tarisa wanted to continue. Once Chris left, she would ask the television for help.

If this were a holiday, a real vacation, Mia would be allowed to watch cartoons for an hour. I would feel no guilt. If that's what she'll want to do while Chris is gone, I'll be fine with the idea.

She imagined Mia watching television from the cot, a picture as if she were looking at the child from behind—a slightly rounded back, a head of black hair, unmoving, like a child numbed to mindlessness.

Enclosed in a ward and emptied out by TV.
But that's not right.

'Can we go home, Mommy?' Mia asked as soon as Chris left.

'Not yet, sweetheart. You still have a fever, a high one.'

They began to chat, finding things outside the window to talk about—the birds, the bus stop, the old mall across the street. Tarisa felt no natural enjoyment, all of it felt effortful, but something in her told her to continue.

She didn't tell Mia that the nurses would soon come in to take her blood. She could tell that Mia was anxious enough just being here. Her silence was not just a sign that she was sick; it was also, Tarisa knew from the way Mia sat up, a sign that she was on alert, that she was concentrating on what she could see, on all the things that might come into this room to terrify her.

'Can we go home, Mommy?'

'We're still going to stay, sweetheart.'

'Why?'

'They have to do a blood test.' The explanation seemed inevitable now.

'Mommy.' Her voice cracked. Mia ground her nose and cheeks on the bedsheet. 'Mommy.'

The repetition brought back memories of Mia tugging her, pulling her arms, and crying, 'Mommy! Mommy! Mommy!' in different places and times. Tarisa had never met any other human who did this: just repeated her name or title without saying anything else, even though that person obviously wanted something specific.

What was it that Mia wanted her to say now?

'Nothing's going to change just because you keep saying, "Mommy". They still have to do the blood test.' Tarisa realized she was beginning to snap.

'Why?'

'Because they need to find out what monsters are in your body.'

'Why?'

'Because they need to find out what monsters are in your body. I don't want to say the same thing over and over again.'

Mia began to cry—a loud, terrible screech.

'And!' Tarisa began, 'Don't you want to heal quickly, for your Little Exhibition at school next Friday?'

'Little Exhibition! Is it tomorrow, Mommy?'

'No, sweetheart, tomorrow's Saturday.' She could feel herself losing her temper. She brought out her fingers to count in a song. 'Saturday, Sunday, Monday, Tuesday, Wednesday, Thursday, Friday.' It was a song that Mia had learned at school and had incidentally taught Tarisa by singing it repeatedly. Mia began to laugh. She brought her fingers out to count along too. 'Let's start again,' Tarisa said, encouraged by Mia's response. They both brought up their fists, slowly unfolding fingers as they counted through the days. Tarisa began to laugh and feel the room fill up with madness.

Mia brightened, as if she had forgotten that something painful was about to happen. 'Are you excited, Mommy?'

'I'm super excited, Mia.'

'Very, very, super excited, Mommy?'

'I'm enthusiastic, Mia.'

'What it means, tusastic?'

'Enthusiastic. It means I'm bursting with excitement. Can you think of another word that means, "very, very excited"?'

'No, Mommy, what?'

Tarisa couldn't think of anything. 'I'm awakened by future-looking, by what the future brings!'

This made Mia laugh. 'More, Mommy, more!'

Tarisa raised her hands to her sides into the air. 'My body's been hit by an epidemic of enthusiasm! For Little Exhibition! For next week's future in your classroom!'

'Me too, Mommy! I'm so, so excited!' Mia put her hands to her cheeks and beamed.

'So! Excited! For this! But first, a blood test!' Tarisa trumpeted, her hands still raised.

Mia frowned and began to cry. Tarisa realized that she had failed. 'Mia, sweetheart, you will be fine.' Tarisa kissed her forehead and pulled her to her chest. Her chin settled on top of Mia's head. They felt blended into one. 'This,' she said, 'is what it feels like to be thinking of the future.'

'Essi—' Mia whispered between her tears. 'Essi what, Mommy?'

'Enthusiastic,' Tarisa whispered, the volatility of the past few minutes unsettling her.

CHAPTER 12

The newcomer disappeared behind the curtains and reappeared cradling a tray heavy with food. Tarisa and Mia had succumbed to the television, which now played a cartoon Tarisa couldn't identify but didn't see as inappropriate. She watched the cartoon with Mia. Doing it as a group activity made her feel less guilty, not like she was leaving her child with some characters she couldn't trust.

The staff placed the tray on the overbed table, where thin, unused borders contoured it like a frame. Her cream mandarin collar blouse glowed like pear meat. She had coloured her eyelids in plum and darkened her lips in crimson, defining the features of her face as if she had a Barbie role model by her mirror. *She is domestic.*

'Good morning,' she said.

'Good morning,' Tarisa replied. She thought that the woman looked familiar. 'Have you said good morning to Auntie, sweetheart? Do you remember Auntie?' she asked Mia, repeating the word 'Auntie' so that Mia wouldn't suddenly refer to her as 'the woman' while she was still in the room.

'No!' Mia said, shaking her head. She dug her face into Tarisa's shirt.

'Sorry. She's just a little bit cranky. Blood test.' Tarisa tried to smile.

'It's okay. You eat your breakfast first and everything will be okay, girl-girl,' the woman said, applying a loose translation of the Mandarin word *mei mei* often used to refer to young girls here.

'Coffee or tea for you, ma'am?' She looked up at Tarisa, smiling while still in a slight bow.

'Coffee, please.'

'Milk and sugar?'

'Just black. Thank you.'

'Mia, look, there's breakfast,' Tarisa said, unwrapping the utensils from the napkin. 'Let's eat.'

Tarisa moved to the sofa with the plate of pineapples and papayas. She chose a slice of pineapple, thinking that it looked like a crown. She imagined herself as a queen eating pineapples. She put the cold fruit in her mouth. The sourness punctured her tongue.

Mia swirled her porridge around for fun. Tarisa kept her eyes on her, making sure she would not spill the food.

She wanted to give the pineapple a good chew. She bit on it slowly and gently, releasing the juice. The sweetness crept to the back of her mouth, sliding down into her throat.

She tried a combination of one piece of pineapple and one piece of papaya. *What happens when you blend the two tastes, crush the papaya slowly, then quickly, then slowly, with your teeth?* The pineapple was fibrous and almost crunchy; the papaya was soft like a cloud. *Cumulonimbus.* Her memories took her back into a carpeted living room, in a one-bedroom apartment with a large television. She and Chris had their feet up and were watching a documentary on cloud-spotting. *What we used to do when life was just us, when we used to relax.*

Tarisa's eyes kept to Mia. Her child was silent, bored, swirling the porridge around again and again. Then, she pierced a piece of papaya with the fork and burrowed it into the porridge.

'Please don't do that,' Tarisa said. 'I want to eat the papaya, not with porridge.'

'I don't like papaya,' Mia said, almost whining.

'I know. But I do. I was gonna eat it.'

'But why, Mommy?' Mia asked.

'Why what?'

'Why you like papaya?'

'It's sweet.' Tarisa wanted this conversation to end. 'Mia, please, I really don't want to eat papaya with porridge.' She left the sofa, approached the overbed table, and lifted the papaya out of the warm porridge, biting her lip.

Gracie suddenly entered with two juniors following her. Bobbling in, one was Geetha. Tarisa did not recognize the other. 'All right, it's time, baby!' Nurse Gracie said. Tarisa did not see any big machine this time. In Geetha's hands were tiny tubes, the ones for Mia's blood to flow into.

'Mommy!' Mia screamed.

Look at the nurses' uniform. It's become green. Last year it was blue. Green: life, safety, growth, more pleasing to the eyes, appetite, and instincts. Look, Mia, you should be enjoying this. Green, Mia. Happy, Mia.

She noticed the singsong voice in her head, the light humour that had suddenly settled in.

Tarisa gave Mia a hug and a smile. 'Gotta do what you gotta do.' Tarisa firmed her grip around Mia's hand.

'It's gonna be ouchie!' Mia said. The saliva between her upper and lower teeth became visible. Tarisa saw in them the strings of a harp, extending long, waiting to be plucked.

Green, Mia. Happy, Mia.

The singsong voice in her head was bothering her. She could not control it or become more serious or fearful, sympathetic.

'Aw, sweetheart,' Tarisa said. 'When I gave birth to you, it was so much more ouchie.'

'Baby, quickly, quickly.' Gracie said.

'Yes, just quickly, and it'll be done, sweetie,' Tarisa said, fully on Nurse Gracie's side.

'We finish this, and after this you can go home,' Nurse Gracie said.

Tarisa snapped around to look at Nurse Gracie. *Bitch.* Her thoughts began to fire. *Do not lie to my daughter. Mia is now hopeful. She thinks she'll go home. 'Didn't the nurse say we could go home?' she will ask as soon as the jab is done, and when I give the answer, she will wonder why we are still here, or worse, why I had not told her the truth. That's going to be more work for me. More talking, more explanations, and Mia might not trust me any more. I need her to trust the things I do.*

'After this, I can go home?' Mia asked.

'Yes, yes, after this you go,' Gracie repeated. The two other nurses took Mia's hands away from Tarisa. Geetha gave Gracie the tube, held Mia's arm out, stretching it. The other nurse rubbed alcohol on her skin, readying it for the puncture.

Tarisa's lips felt hot and wet. She thought of announcing the truth, 'No, Mia, sweetheart, after this, you will still stay here, but it will be fine.' Tarisa tried to look into Gracie's eyes. She hoped to see a message from Gracie—maybe her eyes would ask if what she had just said was okay or maybe they would wink and ask Tarisa to play along. They would, they should, at least acknowledge the lie. *Gracie shouldn't have lied. Gracie should be asking for forgiveness.* Her eyes were radiant, guiltless.

Gracie didn't seem to notice the volatility cutting through Tarisa, who suddenly felt inflamed, shaken in her own body, imagining digging her fingers into Gracie's eyes and pulling out Gracie's tongue and snapping it, making her mouth bleed like a fountain.

No lies. My child will not be lied to. Lies make the world a scary place.

CHAPTER 13

Of course, I could tell Gracie politely, 'Please don't lie. We don't support lying in our family,' or I could laugh and say to Mia, 'No, sweetie. Nurse Gracie's just joking. It'll be at least another night.'

She watched as Gracie tamed Mia.

The words Tarisa imagined wouldn't leave her. Gracie was a figure whom she would need for the next few days: putting medicine in Mia fast, determining what was a medical emergency and what was not. None of these things were things that Tarisa herself could do.

In a way, this room is like my own disempowering cot.

'The environment needs to be sterile, ma'am. You need to leave,' Geetha said.

'It's gonna be ouchie,' Mia said, sobbing.

Tarisa couldn't think about Mia's physical pain. Instead, she thought about the girl's mind, now set up with expectations that she would have to ruin.

'Ma'am, you need to leave,' Geetha repeated, looking stern.

'I'll be right back, sweetheart,' Tarisa said, stroking Mia's head, feeling evicted.

Tarisa stood in front of the closed door. She tried to see what was happening through a small rectangular window, but when she could see only the backs of green uniforms, she gave up on finding images with meaning.

Green, Mia. Happy, Mia.

She could hear herself trying to convince Mia, as if through telepathy, to see the colour of tranquillity the nurses used to cover their skin. This time, she could hear the reduced humour and increased sincerity in her own voice. Mia couldn't hear it, no doubt.

Tarisa was eager to go back inside, but she also felt ashamed, anxious about how to face Mia. She had always taught her, 'No lies. In this family, we always speak the truth.'

'I'm sorry,' she imagined herself saying when they were alone again. 'You're not actually going home.' This would split Mia's reality apart. Mia would begin to see her life in fragments, diagnosing which ones were made from truth, engaging her as an equal partner deserving of honesty, and which ones trilled with lies, with other people's agendas crisscrossing over her head, zooming like paper planes too fast to catch and too unpredictable in their landing.

She should have told Mia what she knew before she had left the room. While stroking her head would have been a good time. She could have whispered it or said it in

Thai. She considered that she had been stroking Mia's head for longer than Geetha could take because she herself could not let go and was trying to send a message through her hands when her lips would not work, torn as they were to hurl an opprobrium towards Gracie instead.

Her head dense with thought, she felt its contours, as if thoughts spread inside and found themselves hitting the interior of her skull. Its oval slopes felt more prominent than usual, a container gentle in its rounded form. She imagined the thickness of her skull—a white, few dense centimetres of uncontrollable rigidity, a basic thing of her humanity that she had no say over but had to rely on silently and instinctively—and the colourful, intentionally constructed environment around that skull now: the walls of the hallway, its lights, the machines that made this the home of medical work.

The photocopy machine at the nurses' station beeped. The phone bleated, waiting for somebody to answer. Two nurses whispered instructions to each other. 'Charge this to the patient.' 'Prepare room for incoming family.' Turning around, letting her back face their room, Tarisa could see the nurses' station. Gracie's lie set in when she saw this: Gracie was part of a set-up of routine—whatever it takes to get the job done, it is only the job that matters. *It's the mom who must deal with the consequences.*

'I want my mommy and daddy! I want to go home!' Mia shouted. Tarisa could hear her. She turned, looking at the door that stayed closed, promising a changed child.

Last year, her sentences were shorter. 'I want Daddy! Mommy!' She's grown.

'You go home now, baby! You go home!' Gracie's voice remained loud and confident. Tarisa could imagine that she was not looking at Mia as she said this. Instead of putting her heart in it to make the child believe her, Gracie would primarily be manoeuvring the tubes and needles that she needed to use on Mia, flinging these words into the air as part of her equipment, letting them land over Mia's head, like a blanket thrown over a child.

CHAPTER 14

Over Gracie's shoulders, Tarisa saw Mia's small face—red, convulsing, booming with a desperate energy. The nurses left, name tags clip-clopping on their thighs. Tarisa read the name of the third one. *Mui. A short, cute name. Like Mia. She's someone's little girl.*

'We go home now, Mommy?' Mia asked in between tears. Tarisa wiped them off with her knuckles, watching her bent fingers cover almost all of Mia's cheeks.

'Let's see what the doctor says, sweetheart.' Tarisa pressed Mia's head to her chest, hoping her heartbeat would soothe the child. *They're gone now. Those bad, lying nurses.*

'You're brave, Mia. You're very brave.' Tarisa kissed the crown of her head, moist with sweat. There, she appeared as wet and helpless as she had in her first few minutes of life outside the womb.

'Are we going home?' Mia asked again. This time, she elongated the 'o', warming it with a nostalgic streak. Tarisa knew where this pronunciation came from: her. Chris had noticed it on one of their first dates in Washington DC.

'I love the way you say home,' he had said. 'It's very cute. *Hoammm.*' Home had been a warm entity, a target of fondness. Tarisa couldn't remember if she said 'home' like this any more, though she must have, if Mia had picked it up. She couldn't imagine it rising with such lustre in the phrases she often used with Mia—'Come on, Mia, let's go home', 'Mia, home'. These sentences raced to get Mia moving, no room to fit fondness in.

'Not yet, sweetie. Not yet. The doctor says two more days here,' Tarisa said, slowly now. There was no rush to move Mia anywhere new. She was not annoyed by the repeated question now either. She heard in it denial, a child's kind, which softened the value of the preceding moment with no attempt at self-deception, only hope that the past and the future might be disconnected elements of a vast, barely sensible world.

'Why?'

'Because we have to get the monsters out of you.'

'But why?'

'Because we have to get the monsters out of you.' She noticed her own repetition, her own lack of need to say something new. 'There are little monsters inside of you, and we'll get them out.'

'I want to go home.' Mia elongated the 'o' again.

'You're sick and an in-patient. The doctor says you still can't go.'

Mia didn't seem to wonder about the contradiction between Gracie's message and what Tarisa was saying now.

Relieved that she had dodged a difficult conversation, she sat down beside Mia, feeling close, noticing that the child might actually like home.

And if that's what Mia already thought was good, then she had been cheated. A good place should be so much more, one with excited mothers waiting eagerly for their children. Here you are, restricted to your cot unless I help you move around. You are here because of me.

'Where's Daddy, Mommy?'

'Home, sweetheart.'

'Why Daddy can go home?'

'He's not the sick one, sweetie.' *You're maybe not sick enough to be here either.* 'I wonder why he's taking so long. Home's not far from here.'

She could not imagine Chris just lying somewhere doing nothing. Since Mia's birth, Tarisa had never seen him staring into space. He was often, if not always, doing something with Mia, playing the piano, reading, or sleeping.

She could not imagine him using the luxury of aloneness to read. The piano, perhaps he could be playing, certain that no noise would disrupt the sacred sounds of his music. Sleep, this one was unlikely, since he would tell himself that sleep was not possible when there was sunshine.

It's the piano then?

Yet, she could not imagine him making music, pressing melodies into keys when his child was in a hospital. There would need to be serenity to make the kind of jazz that he does, climbing up and down scales with an adventurer's thirst.

But maybe that was not right.

Tarisa imagined him walking around in the apartment alone, having his own relationship with it. Maybe he had a very different way of being that she had never gotten to know.

At almost noon, Mia's body called for a nap. Tarisa patted her as they both laid down on the cot, nearly spooning. She, too, was falling asleep, letting a dream begin.

The door cracked open. Tarisa wanted to slam it shut.

'Hey guys, I'm back!' Chris said, removing his backpack. Tarisa realized it was too late to raise her finger to her lips. She quickly glanced at Mia, whose eyes were closed, fluttering, like they were chewing sleep.

'Got the stuff. You can check if anything's missing,' he said quietly, now that Tarisa had pointed to a sleeping Mia.

'I'm sure nothing's missing. A meticulous man went in search for the stuff.'

He chuckled. 'Feel free to go take a walk.'

'Have you had anything to eat?'

'Just quickly made oatmeal at home.'

Her alertness heightened. She'd want to think seriously about their lunch in that case. Oatmeal was a sign that Chris was being utilitarian. Although he could be practical about many things for long, his bond with good food was not whimsical but habitual. If he did not eat something decent for the next meal or so, he would begin to act like an irritated baby.

'There's some pineapple if you want some. I saved some for you. From breakfast. It's in the fridge.' It was the best she could do for now.

'Oh, yeah, are you sure? If you're not eating it, I might. Thanks.'

That he accepted immediately signalled to her that she had guessed correctly: He had not found satisfaction in the oatmeal. She could imagine him cradling it to his mouth, then pushing it in, like a man spoon-feeding himself, knowing he must acquire calories and nutrients.

The image scared her. She didn't want to think about the Chris who was dissatisfied right now, in this hospital room. Physically, she did not feel threatened. He was not the type to take out his irritation on her by yelling or hurting her, as she had told Mia when comparing him to the Uzbek man squeezing a woman's neck in the backseat of a car. And yet, what was at stake still, was her happiness. If he could not be happy in this hospital, then her own happiness would have to be subdued, and happiness subdued was not quite happiness after all.

She wanted to test how he felt some more.

'Well, I would eat it, but I want you to eat it because you probably want to eat it. You like pineapples. I want to express my love to you, so I'm giving you pineapples that I also want. That's my show of love,' she said.

'Oh, okay, thanks.'

She thought a more promising response would have been him coming toward her with a kiss or phrases like, 'I love you, too. Thank you.' She even imagined some back and forth, some pushing and pulling of the symbolic pineapple between them. *'No, you can have the pineapple.'*

'No, you, please.' 'No, you.' 'No, you.' 'Thank you, I appreciate what you are doing for me.'

It worried her that he didn't do this. What if it was more than the oatmeal at home? Was he already finding this ward terrible?

Please, don't. It's too soon. I'm just beginning to relax.

'Do you *not* want them?' she asked.

Maybe he's not even troubled. He probably overate the oatmeal. Maybe he's just not hungry or interested in talking about food right now.

Because normal people would do that.

Normal people would also not overthink this.

'I want them, but later,' he said.

Tarisa paused and nodded her head while looking around at the floor.

'Feel free to go out,' he said again.

She was enjoying it here and hadn't thought about leaving. There was a calmness that she appreciated. She wanted to just sit on the sofa and be with them both in this animal warmth.

He wasn't repeating this to push her out or be impolite. He was just trying to be nice, she knew. He wanted her to get to wherever she wanted to be.

She considered a walk for the sake of exercise. A walk could be good to stretch her legs, for they had been in a cot for hours, and they would be there again tonight, scrunched up as she tried to sleep. And perhaps she could get him something good to eat, and even to read. She would go to the library, then pick up food on the way back.

'I'll go. Do you want anything from the library?' She, too, could get a copy of Tanizaki's novel, which she had forgotten to bring and forgotten to put on the list of things she had wanted Chris to bring from home.

'Oh, no, it's okay. I brought some books from home. Thanks.' He walked to his backpack and pulled out a hardcover: *Playing Changes: Jazz for the new century*. He placed the book on the desk and drummed his fingers on it as if he were with his piano. She had seldom seen him pass on the opportunity to read something new, especially when access to books was so close.

Perhaps the oatmeal is really dragging him down.

'If it's better, I could *not* go to the library and save my going-out quota for dance tonight,' she said, wanting to show that she was here for him.

'No, no, you should go. You should go to the library *and* dance.'

'Then you should go out one more time, too. Take a break as much as me.'

'No, that's silly. It's okay. It doesn't work like that.'

'Equality works like that.'

'No, no. It's more complicated than that. You should just go to the library. Then tonight, you go and dance.'

'Are you *sure*? I really can skip the library, stay here with you.'

He didn't say anything for a few seconds.

'No. No need to skip anything. Just go to the library.' He looked at the ground and chuckled.

'Okay.' She paused. That chuckle made her see that he was not entirely downcast. 'I'll change and go to the library. Are you *sure* you don't want anything?'

'No,' he said, and finally reached for the pineapples.

When he finished eating, Chris brought out her hyaluronic acid, moisturizer, and vitamin C serum from his backpack and placed them on the dressing table. She took them to the bathroom, placing each item carefully on the tiny countertop, which couldn't comfortably hold everything. It might have seemed excessive to stick to her skincare routine during a hospital stay, but she didn't want to break the discipline. Guilt would override her, tell her to do more after she had started breaking out, which was happening since she'd quit her last job—*There must have been something that changed my hormones after becoming a stay-at-home mother.* Now, she would do anything to revive her skin. Maybe it was part of what would make him want her again. He had complimented her—'Your skin looks radiant. I can't stop looking at you'—in her second trimester. *Clearly, he can feel attracted, he can identify beauty. He just cannot fuck.*

She lumped the bottles together so that none would fall. The bathroom came to look more like the one at home.

She washed her face. She looked up at a burgeoning pimple and imagined what it would have been like to go to the office with breakouts, and she was, for a brief second, grateful for this life where she had nowhere to go but school and home.

And imagine showing up at the World Economic Forum like this.

Shut up, that sounds like self-pity.

But nothing wrong with a little self-pity. Look at what's happened to you.

She began to apply the hyaluronic acid. She paced around in the bathroom as she waited for it to seep into her pores. She didn't like the pimple and wanted to burst it before it grew into anything bigger, but she held back. She remembered that the best thing to do was to wait for it to dry out or wait for someone who properly knew how to remove it for her. Either way, waiting was a necessary part of the process. She tapped brown and rose-gold eyeshadow onto her eyelids and drew on warm, brown eyeliner, trying to distract herself from focusing on the pustule.

She stepped out of the bathroom, feeling like it was now her duty to go out, now that she had put on makeup, and looked for the time: half past noon. Mia was napping, a thumb in her mouth. Chris was reading the jazz book. Sunshine splashed onto the pages, coming in through the window, as if the sun, too, wanted a book to have and to hold.

Lunch soon. The nurses will come in. Mia will wake up for medicine. There's always medicine around lunchtime.

Tarisa had pre-ordered steamed fish and fried rice. It was the tastiest and most nutritious item on the menu. If Chris was hungry, he could eat that. *I'll also remember to get him something from outside.* She didn't want to tell him yet that she had had this thought. A surprise would be better. Surprises inherently made no promises, so if what she tried was imperfect, he still would, not knowing what went wrong, say thank you.

CHAPTER 15

The streets were hot with sunshine.

The café she used to help at was near here. She walked over and thought about stopping by to say hello to her friend, the owner, but it looked like only his new staff members were there. She didn't know any of them, so she continued towards the library. This was the road that she had walked on four years ago, right after the doctor had confirmed that she was pregnant.

When the news came, she was in the café. She answered the doctor's call. 'Congratulations, you're pregnant,' he said, while she was standing behind rows of hardened bread for the purposes of display, readjusting pencils and order forms, which the lunch crowd had messed up knowing she would clean up after them. No one knew, and she didn't expect them to, that she was here, now waitressing, because there was nothing more for her to do in Singapore.

'I'm pregnant!' she shouted to her friend.

She didn't know yet that the day Mia was conceived would be the last time they would ever have sex.

Her friend came out of the kitchen, throwing his apron off. 'Go! Go home! No more of this!' He waved his arms up and down, then jutted his belly out at her. 'You're pregnant now! Congrats!'

She hugged him, but not too tightly, careful about her stomach. 'Thanks so much for the time here,' she said. 'If I hadn't interviewed you for the food magazine, we wouldn't have met, and I would be bored at home right now. Thanks for giving me a chance for these past few months.'

The food magazine she had written for was horrible: the boss cursed a lot and asked people if they had asked their 'father's dick' their questions before asking him. The door opened and closed for quitters and their replacements every month.

'No, seriously, it's waitressing,' her friend said, trying to be modest, though it hurt her feelings.

For a second, she forgot about the pregnancy.

'Better than nothing on this island that seems to have been made for finance and economics people. I don't even know why I'm here.' She hung her apron and left, walking past money changers and bankers. The people around her didn't seem to matter. A more ethereal force picked up her feet and made her glide.

She dialled Chris' number as she passed the bakeries filled with sweets and donuts, considering having one, or a few. 'Pregnant!' she shouted as soon as he answered.

'Whoa!' She could hear him trying to keep himself together. 'T, that's amazing! This is big news!'

She agreed. She had experienced nothing this exciting for several months, and because she did not understand how far from independence, reason, and a homeostatic state of calm babies were, she did not think about the coming downsides. It was a naïve understanding of parenthood, the kind of ignorance that comes easily to people who didn't grow up around babies, who moved from one place to another before they could become somebody meaningful enough for new parents to show their babies to for hours on end.

'Wait, the bus is here. I'm gonna have to hang up. But yay! See you soon, Daddy!'

He laughed when she said this. She could tell that his happiness was real.

On the bus, passing green fields, she stared out the large window. There were two worlds at once. She saw a baby crawling between her lap and Chris'. She also saw a man mowing the fields with a sharp metal cutter. The baby in her head smiled so sweetly. Dead leaves flew at the bus window. She heard Chris' laughter in her imagination. The leaves smacked the glass. When she tried to look at the cutter's blades to see how long they were, she could only see something moving so fast that it looked like a blooming flower. She hoped the flower wouldn't slice open the operator's legs.

She got off the bus carefully, planting her feet firmly on the ground one at a time, the way she thought a pregnant woman should take care of her body. She thought about yelling to the driver as a half-joke, 'Careful, I'm pregnant!'

At a quarter past five, she was waiting behind the apartment door, leaving enough space for Chris to swing it open without hitting her stomach. When she heard the door code being punched, the glow from her belly rose to her face. He opened the door and saw her standing there, shining. They both opened their arms, and she dived straight into his chest. She arched her back when their bodies came together so that they wouldn't suffocate the zygote.

Leela, who had had Tarisa at the same age, cried over the phone when she heard the news. They told her they had a name for a baby if it was going to be a girl. 'Mia,' they said together. 'After Mamma Mia,' Tarisa continued. 'Because a stranger at the airport one day said to Chris, back when I was in Berkeley, "*Mamma Mia!* You fly from Washington to California to see each other every other weekend?"'

Tarisa hadn't been diligent about trying to conceive. She had unprotected sex with Chris and said that if the baby came, it came. Since her life had been thrown off by 'that October' anyway, she was entertaining all possible variables, including parenthood. It seemed like the timing would make sense. Plus, or maybe because of that, her hormones had been encouraging her. When she saw pregnant women, she rubbed her belly in envious sympathy.

Chris, aware of his worsening erectile dysfunction, gave every session of sex his fullest dedication. He wanted to become a father. He relied on tadalafil from Thailand—no need for a prescription—to make his erections work, and as far as Tarisa was concerned, the sex was efficient.

It was good enough to make her hopeful that she could become a mother too.

Now, walking on the streets, four years after the conception, she felt the sun's heat on her, like a bad song that would never end. She squinted at another mother nearby, waiting with her children at the traffic light. She thought about whether the children were even wanted. Tarisa recalled a time when she and Chris had been going over how Mia's existence came about.

'INTJ. What did you get?' she was saying, looking at the website Sixteen Personalities on her phone and rubbing her belly, which held Mia inside.

'ISFJ,' he said, looking at his own screen, sitting legs crossed on the couch, to avoid her belly. He was afraid of accidentally kicking and killing Mia. 'The Defender. Apparently,' his fingers signalled air quotes, '"quite unique".' The sum of their parts opposed their individual definitions. 'However sensitive, defenders analyse situations excellently; however reserved, they have robust relationships and people skills; however conservative, defenders have a high ability to welcome change and new ideas,' he read.

'Sounds kind of right. You *have* changed a lot since that October. You now believe,' Tarisa said in a mock-journalist voice, 'in invisible sexism, that it can happen even between loving husband and wife, thanks to your wife's explanations and your own listening.' She had spent the weeks before her pregnancy explaining to him, in a manner she thought was rational, how what had happened that October was a result of his gendered socialization.

'I don't think I would have ever done that to you. I don't think that, as a woman, I ever grew up thinking, "I'll just uproot someone suddenly and say I can pay for the rest of their life, so it should be fine for them that their dreams won't be fulfilled." I think you did it because you've seen many men do it.' She could not stop. 'Many men just assume they'll lead the household financially, and if they can lead financially, then they should just lead everything, and their wives should be fine with that,' she said, rambling but firm. Her truths had come to feel important, no longer extraneous factors to hide.

'Yeah, ISFJ does sound accurate. What about yours?'

'INTJ,' she said, taken aback. From the way he quickly tried to divert their attention, she guessed that he still was still uncomfortable with what could be said between them. She tried to help him by talking about what he wanted to, cooling the potential flare. Her point had already been made, no need to belabour. 'INTJs are often introverted and would be more partial to a set-up where they get to work alone. People with this personality type are able to focus on the big picture and are more likely to pay attention to abstract information rather than the multitude of actual details. INTJs usually think that rationale, logic, and objective information are of greater import than subjective emotions. People with this personality type like to feel in control and therefore seek to impose order in their world by making plans well in advance,' she read, grateful that there were many lines she could read while the back of her mind tried to digest his discomfort.

'Sounds pretty accurate.'

'Yeah. Although I might argue that it was hormones more than logic that led to this,' she said, looking at her pregnancy. 'Remember how I was rubbing my belly in February whenever I saw a pregnant woman, like I wanted to be her?'

He nodded.

'No regrets,' she said. She thought about the future that was about to come, a future that was recently designed for her. 'This should be fine even if I'm going back to work. And, like, real work this time. My kind of work—research. Research again. I'm excited for this new job, Chris. Thankful that the professors from Harvard referred me. No more food-writing gigs. No more waitressing. This job's real, and it's gonna last.'

The only job that would last was the one taking care of Mia. I was too naïve, she thought now, looking at her shadow being stomped on by other pedestrians.

She knew, for a long time, that she loved Chris, that she loved them. They were, more than half, her chosen family. Chris was fully chosen. Mia was half chosen. As a concept of a child, she was chosen; as herself, Mia wasn't. Tarisa had two members of a family who averaged out to be seventy-five per cent her choice. *Not too bad. Many women have it at zero per cent.* Tarisa had never thought about her family mathematically, but those percentages, calculated under a traffic light, now reassured her that this was the life she had wanted.

'Be quiet! Can't you just be quiet!' a mother tugging her children said, pulling Tarisa away from her daydreams. She was in jean shorts and a cartoon t-shirt. In a way, she looked like an enlarged child.

Maternal anger builds up over time. Anxiety, stress, fatigue, all bundled into one body that is expected to consistently perform at the standard of angels. Motherhood can be—is not always, but can be—the recipe for the destruction of a human.

How did this woman's two children come along? They looked like they were two or three years apart.

Those years should have given this mother, this kind of mother, enough time to understand the onerousness of children. Why was the second child there? Was it a mistake? The result of societal pressure? 'Why don't you have two? You should have two!'

Tarisa could imagine strangers nudging the mother to produce more. Strangers did it to her. From taxi drivers to supermarket cashiers, people who discovered that Mia had no siblings talked to Tarisa about the disservice that she was doing. One taxi driver told her that she was 'killing' Mia. 'You have one child means you kill it.' Colourful taxis in primary colours raced by her on the streets now. She saw the drivers, old, middle-aged men, and wondered how many children they had had, and had made their wives raise.

Even before these strangers in Singapore, she had grown up hearing that having just one child was considered a deficit. 'Two is about right. One is too little,' her parents had said, before she asked them to 'really stop'.

'What about three?' she asked her father once—not intending to have three, but rather seeking to understand how people who calculated the ideal number of children thought.

'Three should be the maximum,' he said with certainty. 'Otherwise, you just look like you have a dangling posse.'

Tarisa thought that the mother struggling with her two children now looked like she already had a dangling posse. The crosswalk light turned green. Tarisa followed behind them, slowing down to observe. She watched as the mother dragged her children by the arms, the way one would drag cumbersome luggage at an airport, eagerly waiting to get rid of it at check-in. The children's Velcro shoes grazed the asphalt before they lifted their feet up for kicks rising to their mouths, damaging the soundwaves of their own screams.

Men and women carrying shopping bags passed by without seeming to notice. Tarisa thought about the limp child on the train whom she had seen just over twenty-four hours earlier, sighing at the commonness of hurt children.

'Boom,' Tarisa said under her breath, imagining that their mother had let go of their hands, dropping them to the street, where a sedan crashed into one of them, then the other one, who would be screaming before being hit too. 'Boom,' she whispered again. She reached the other side of the road.

As soon as they saw the library door, the children began to run, leaving their mother behind. She did not run after them, the way one would not run after luggage that was travelling away on a conveyer belt, only to be reunited hours later.

The library took the children in. The automatic door shut before she reached it, then reopened for her. Tarisa followed, trading in her shadow for air-conditioning and books. From the way the mother moved calmly now, it was difficult to imagine her doing what she had just done with the children.

That's what they say about sociopaths.

That's how nice people think I am and how I really am with Mia.

~~~

She quickly passed through the lobby, not greeting the staff or taking a look at the magazines they had put out for visitors to browse. She considered that greeting them could be helpful to herself—it would liven up her mood, give her a chance to look at somebody and exchange some smiles. Yet, she didn't. *This is not how it is done in this country, except as exceptions.* She could try and hope to be reciprocated with an exception. By the time she had gotten to this point of her thought process, she had already walked far away from the lobby. It was too late to smile now—what she realized she had wanted to do.

Tarisa descended into the basement, strolling down the escalators while older men in tattered clothing stood on one side, grabbing onto the handrails, chewing on toothpicks, or jingling coins in their pockets. She had never picked up the habit of standing on escalators, no matter how long they were or whether their trajectory was upwards or downwards.

She planned to head to the children's area first. The adult books were on the same floor, but Tarisa wanted to get Mia a book before scanning the aisles for herself. Children's books were usually lighter; it would be easier for her to carry them as she browsed for Tanizaki and perhaps a few other titles, as opposed to the other way around. She was honest with herself about not attending to Mia first for any other reason.

She had never been to the children's area without Mia. She thought of mothers who regularly went out without the children *for* them, the mothers who embodied a momentum of living for their kids, as if a rush of anxious nurturing erected their spines and greased their limbs. She had seldom, if ever, found herself so mobilized.

She thought about the popcorn from the previous morning. *Didn't I buy Mia just that one bag, nothing more? It was also a flavour that Chris and I preferred. The plan was to have Mia eat whatever we wanted to eat ourselves.* And now, she realized that Mia hadn't even eaten it. She had forgotten to ask for it once they had got home, and Tarisa had also forgot to offer it again.

Maybe Mia will forget about it by the time we get home.
I could eat it myself then, when she goes back to school.
If she remembers after it's gone, I'll tell her it expired.

Inside, the geometric carpeting grew like an endless kaleidoscope, flourishing without the usual stampede of little feet. She didn't see the mothers who were often here with their infants, shuttled in strollers or slings. Tarisa had often wondered where they went together all day long. When Mia was that age, a day alone with her seemed like an impossible amount of time to fill.

She spotted the family that had just crossed the street with her. The two children had changed the expressions of their faces, now looking lush and colourful, the rounds of their cheeks popping out like buns, now that wide, screaming mouths weren't pushing and pulling on their skin. The mother, looking fatigued as before, fished for her phone in her pocket and found a spot on a bench with no books nearby.

The siblings plucked books off the shelves, piled them into their arms, and climbed into a treehouse in the centre of the children's area. *I see why two is a good number. It leaves the mother alone.* They threw the books onto the floor. The older sibling snatched one back up, opened it, and beamed at the pictures before the other joined, packing their heads together, laughing at words only one could read. Soon, the older sibling ran into a word he did not know. From hearing his attempts—'kunf', 'konvee'—Tarisa guessed the word was either 'comfy' or 'conversation'.

'Mommy, Mommy, read!' Looking down from the tree house, he shouted to his mother. She did not look up from her phone. She was a familiar shape—reclined onto a chair, neck slanted, staring into a phone. The boy brought over the book; his sibling waited on top. He repeated, trying to make eye contact, 'Mommy, Mommy, read to me.' He tried to put the book near his mother's face, but she whacked it away. Tarisa wanted to read to him.

Without Mia here, it would be bizarre if she did. If Mia were around, she could do this naturally. The other children would come to sit around them while Tarisa read to Mia, and Tarisa would turn up her volume, while their parents' fingers squirreled around on oil-slicked phones. She had done this before, with Mia noticing and asking her why other children were there too. She had answered, in Thai, to not hurt their feelings, 'Because not all parents read to their children who want to hear stories. We can share our story, sweetheart'—a response that Mia didn't take to, saying, 'Their mommies can read to them.'

Tarisa tried to suppress her agony now as she listened to the boy plead for his mother's attention. She touched the spines of books on display, searching for traces of wood in spines bent and browned, to distract herself. Yet, even with her back turned to him, she could feel her listening move towards him with sympathy. She tried to reason with herself, to find the sympathy for the mother, too. This might be her only couple of minutes of respite, her neglect of her children her moment of self-care.

Then, suddenly, a selfish thought struck: if she prepared Mia to go into the world with intelligence and confidence, these children, who were raising themselves to be wailers and whimperers in a climate of neglect, would be at her feet. *I could easily build Mia to get to the top. Look at the instinct that's kicking in. My sympathy for other children doesn't even last for long.* She chuckled, as softly as she had whispered 'boom' on the streets. The child still in the treehouse began to howl. She watched his neck elongate as his chin made its way towards the ceiling. His lips gathered almost into a pucker, as all of his mouth turned into a hose spraying a howl into the children's area, onto stories meant to be shared.

Disturbed by the sound, made longer and longer, Tarisa told herself to grab a book and quickly leave—but it couldn't be just any book. She looked to her left, where the Comic Sans sign read '0–3 years', then to her right: '4–6 years'. She stepped towards the latter because Mia no longer read like a three-year-old.

She picked up a book on flowers because she and Mia knew little about them. She wanted a book that would enrich Mia's world and her own, nothing more about princesses. She decided to borrow it, however, because it looked like it would be the most convenient to read. Each page had only a picture of a flower and its common name. There were twenty-six pages, each naming a flower. This meant that she would be speaking very little and that she wouldn't be bothered with any questions about plot. The flowers bloomed beautifully, unlike the stained, wilted pages they sat on.

Tarisa was ready to find *A Companion*. She didn't dislike nonfiction, but fiction attracted her more. Someone else's reality didn't seem like a necessary thing to know. Life was a secluded journey, the throngs of people who never gave her any interaction proof that disinterest was a common human goal. She pivoted towards the aisles where old men usually sat sleeping, in a nest of stories they barely touched.

She remembered that around here, she had written a note to herself on her phone two years ago, when she had come to this same spot with Chris and Mia. It was strange to think now that she and Chris had once accompanied their one-year-old to the library together. He could have taken care of Mia alone; she hadn't needed to join them. She could vaguely remember why she was also present: if she had stayed home, all she would have done was watch YouTube or taken a nap. Back then, she still thought that she should feel guilty doing either.

She wanted to see what she had written for a sense of how she used to be. She knew that there had been progress, from then to now. In an unnamed folder in her phone, still standing, she found the notes she had penned here, in the past.

He's left the aisle and taken her somewhere, strolling, probably. She's probably fallen asleep. When I told him I sometimes imagined her dead, it didn't go too well. I am somewhere, but it is not a place.

I see them now through an aisle. She is awake with a book she isn't reading. It's in her hand like a prop, and sitting around are all the men I imagined killed her. There are about twenty of them. That's about twenty ways to kill.

The truth is not that. They now sit lazily in armchairs, snoring or reading. (Where are the women? Do they not sleep in libraries?)

She turned the screen off after this question, feeling what she often felt when she decided to cut off from it: like leaving her phone could only ever be temporary.

She remembered that her thumbs had crushed these words into her phone, as if she had remembered that a phone was a place to throw her heaviness out. Of course, there was no such thing as throwing it out. Merely externalizing it was what she did. She didn't know herself well enough yet, the guilt and anger still causing more confusion than a sense of identity, and therefore, she needed to write to see who or what she was.

Now, she was not the woman who had written that note. She did not imagine Mia dying any more. Her current life was bearable because of the existence of school days. A few hours of alone time in a day had allowed her to see that she should not be confused, but understanding that as not-a-mother she is one person, and as a mother, she is another. One felt liberated, at ease, in pursuit of fulfilling things, more than the other. She had never been so bored or felt so stuck in her life until she was with Mia all day, every day, especially then, when she was a blob of flesh that needed to be carried around and leaked liquids from all sorts of orifices at disruptive intervals.

She sat down on the couch where she had written the paragraphs to re-enact the scene, trying to remember how her fingers had moved irritably. Her thumbs jived, stomping in the air above the black screen seated in her fingers, which curled around it like a butterfly's antennae in children's drawings. No words came to her mind.

She lit up the screen again and scrolled to the bottom of the note to see what she would type now if she really had a place to put words again, but nothing came out. Her fingers only hovered, until the screen turned off on its own. She saw her own reflection and wiggled her eyebrows up and down, greeting and playing with herself.

She got up to find the Tanizaki novel, knowing the process would be quick. The process of discovery there was different from finding Mia's books: it would be finding a book where the author's name had been shelved alphabetically, not opening the pages to see if threats of inconvenient contents were inside. Soon, Tanizaki's pages curved in her hands, like a tunnel she could go through. She placed the width of the book, gently rounded in her hands, to her eye, and aimed her sight at the exit.

Leaving, she looked back one more time at the men who sat sleeping on the couches. One stood out, his eyes open. He wasn't doing anything, wasn't playing with a phone. He seemed at peace with where he was. Calm people looked like that, like there was a frame around them and they were comfortably seated in it.

She fanned herself with the Tanizaki as soon as the main exit doors sliced open, and could hear the pages wobbling.

She still needed to get wonderful food for Chris, who wouldn't be happy eating two practical meals in a row. She wanted to get him a gift that would seem a little spectacular. One little gesture, one at a time, to keep him going at the hospital. Normally, he went for a box of six takoyaki, so Tarisa calculated and decided that she would get ten pieces now.

As she walked, she remembered that a few steps away, just in front of the mall, where cars entered and exited the parking lot, she had almost accidentally killed Mia when she had just been a year old. She had been pushing Mia's stroller and had dropped a water bottle. She then bent down to pick it up, thinking that she had pressed the lock lever. But when she looked up, Mia was rolling into the street. She managed to get to the stroller just before the light turned green, allowing cars to come through.

She told herself to be kind to herself for making such mistakes. After all, being with a child all day long provided much room for error. It was, she tried to convince herself with calculations she knew she should doubt, only a matter of probability. *The more you are with an infant, the more chances you have to accidentally kill it.*

She didn't tell Chris until a year later that this had happened. Standing with a dining table between them, a dining table they were both clearing, she told him with doe eyes and rooted confidence that this episode did not matter. The effect she wanted to produce was of an afterthought. *Chris, the fact that an accident had happened is an afterthought to how it doesn't matter. Mia is still alive.* His response was a low hum—of recognizing the factual negligibility of the accident, of shock that it had happened, or of acceptance that this is the kind of mother she had become; she couldn't discern which. She looked at the space hung between his low hum and her, not knowing if his reticence was ideal and judging that what was happening was perhaps neutrality.

She announced the arrival of takoyaki when she entered the hospital room by holding the box up to her face, to which she added a smile, hoping that she could also amplify her own happiness. 'Takoyaki!' she said, in impeccable Japanese from her days of studying Comparative Literature. She tightened her grip the on the two books underneath the takoyaki box.

'Oh, thanks!' Chris said, the tail of his voice lifting energetically. She hadn't seen him so happy since—

—she couldn't remember.

She placed the two books down on the desk while Chris changed Mia into a new set of patient uniforms.

'What happened to the old one?' she asked.

'Oh, she puked a little bit on it. The nurses came to give her medicine, and she was crying and puked a little.'

'*They* didn't change the uniform?'

'Oh, no, they said they would, but I just said I'd do it myself.'

'Why?'

'No, nothing. Just thought I could do it myself.'

Tarisa raised her eyebrows.

'Also, since she had a lot of trouble taking the medicine, they said they would ask the doctor what to do. Mia was spitting it out again and again. They're looking at an IV drip.'

'Gracie didn't just shove it in like last time? With a syringe?'

'She tried, but Mia's getting too big for that. She was fighting Gracie just now. Almost bit the syringe. It's too dangerous.'

She liked how matter-of-fact he sounded, an indicator that he was able to see the medical necessity of being here supersede the ways the inconveniences might have bothered him.

IV drips weren't Tarisa's preference. They were a nuisance when Mia needed to use the bathroom. The plug would need to be disconnected from its charge, Mia would need to be reminded to walk slowly, and a parent would need to make sure they followed her carefully for her to not trip over the cord.

Tarisa placed the takoyaki on the overbed table, which Chris appeared to have already moved towards the couch, sliding the lunch tray that was filled with leftovers a few inches away. She stuck a skewer in one of the takoyaki immediately. Chris appreciated them at this temperature, exactly. 'You should eat it now. It's just right, warm,' she said.

He quickly finished putting on Mia's clothes and gravitated to the couch, in front of the food. 'Mia, you want some?' he asked, picking up the box and tilting it towards her.

'No, I don't like it,' Mia said.

'You've never tried it,' Tarisa said.

'Yes, but I don't like it,' Mia said.

'Want some?' Chris asked Tarisa.

'No, thank you. All yours.' She began to pick at the hospital leftovers—steamed fish, fried rice, stir-fried vegetables. *But Mia should have wanted fried rice.* 'Mia, you didn't want the fried rice?' Tarisa pointed to pieces of sausage in it.

Mia shook her head.

'You're gonna be hungry, you know,' Tarisa said.

'I don't want it.'

'What are you gonna do when you're hungry?'

'You can buy something for me.'

Tarisa raised her eyebrows and looked away. *Like I would when you've got this.*

Chris blew on the takoyaki to cool it. Then, he took a small bite, just enough to shake up the sphere into something more deflated. She imagined how she would instead inhale the entire ball. What he did seemed like an instinctive precaution, even though Tarisa had just said it was 'just right, warm'. She worried over how he didn't seem to trust her judgment.

'So good,' he said.

'I'm glad,' Tarisa said.

'I don't like it,' Mia said.

'No one asked,' Tarisa said under her breath. '*You can buy something for me.' How entitled.* Only Chris heard her aside and chuckled.

'What?' Mia asked.

'Nothing. I was talking to your dad.'

'What you say?'

'I said—' Tarisa couldn't think of anything fast enough. 'Ugh, I don't know. What *did* I say?'

'She forgot,' Chris said. Tarisa gave him a quick, hidden smile that said thank you.

'You forgot?' Mia asked, looking at her mother.

'I forgot,' Tarisa said. Chris looked back at her with a hidden smile, too. She appreciated how he didn't judge her for every way she did motherhood incorrectly.

Chris ate the rest of the takoyaki, blowing each one, while Mia sat flipping through books that Chris had brought from home. Rubbing his belly, which drew Tarisa's attention to his limp penis underneath, he got up from the sofa, coming towards Tarisa as she stood by the desk, reshuffling and organizing miscellany into neat piles. Chris touched her waist and pouted his lips. She raised her head towards his and gave him a peck. The desire to kiss him was returning, stronger and stronger, as she noticed his mood become lighter here.

'I'll take a shower,' he said.

'Take your time.'

'Thank you,' he said, then went into the bathroom.

'Mommy, can you read to me?' Mia asked as soon as they were alone. She pointed to a book with unicorns and princesses, a book Tarisa already knew, and knew to be twenty pages long, with a couple of sentences on each page.

'What about this?' Tarisa said right away, grabbing the library book next to the now-organized miscellany and standing it on its edges, so that its flower-adorned cover would pull Mia in.

'Wow!' Mia said and held out both hands. Tarisa fed them the book. She thought again about how it wouldn't have appealed to Mia in the library, but here, now, there was little else to excite her.

Tarisa went to sit by her side. She opened the book so that the first page Mia would see would be after the title page. Tarisa didn't want to be asked to read information on copyright, the publisher, or the rights of the author and the illustrator, which Mia, constantly excited by text, would ask her to do.

'Amaranthus,' Tarisa read the first word, pointing to the bright flower drooping down. Her finger travelled to the adjacent page. 'Baby's Breath.'

'*Baby's* breath,' Mia said. '*Baby's* breath,' she repeated, giggling.

'Maybe because it looks so small and delicate, like the breath of little babies? Do you think your breath looks like these little flowers, Mia?' She caught herself. Even though she had thought that she wouldn't want to talk much to Mia—the point of this book—she was already doing something unplanned.

It might be because I feel pretty happy right now.
I feel happy because I successfully skipped over the copyright page.
'I'm not so sure,' Mia said.
Happy feels nice.

'I think they might. Because you're so small,' Tarisa said, swirling her finger in a tiny circle around Mia's belly. She watched it move, curling and curling. *This feels good. Let it continue.* 'And the breaths that come out of your little lungs might be so tiny like this.'

'Maybe.'

'Maybe.'

They travelled through the pages together, looking at drawings of flowers blooming. The happiness continued as each page powered Tarisa's feelings of being a present and productive mother, while having to do no more than read a name on a page.

Tarisa was surprised by some of the names— Narcissus, Quaker Ladies—but she held back her surprise. She didn't want to unseam Mia's curiosity and trap herself in explanation. Surely, if she did not show clues that something was interesting, Mia wouldn't realize that it was. Although she wanted them to have a good time, Narcissus' and the Quakers' stories were long, not anything that could swiftly quench Mia's encyclopaedic thirst.

'Can we read it again, Mommy?' Mia said when they finished at Zenobia.

She would just be reading twenty-six short names again. 'Sure, sweetheart, we can,' she said with a smile. Mia opened the cover of the book again, with the same eager tempo as the first time, while Tarisa surreptitiously tacked the copyright page towards the cover again.

'A book about flowers?' Chris asked, coming out of the bathroom, his hands bundling his old clothes.

'Yes,' Tarisa said. 'A book with only names. Only twenty-six names.' She turned to him and grinned, giving him an understanding of what she meant. He smiled to show he understood. She quietly remembered the mother and the children whom she had seen at the library just an hour ago. She was not so bad, reading twenty-six names, compared to that woman.

As soon as she thought this, she shook her head. *No, no. Don't compare. It's all meant to be different. Be kind to her. Mothers are all different. This, you should already know.*

Tarisa looked at the clock, the smooth gliding of its hands pacifying her. In three hours, she would be at her movement class with Edwina, a dancer who had just finished a world tour and was now back in Singapore. Tarisa did not know if the next three hours would pass by as quickly as the last ten minutes had, reading the flower book twice, pausing for Mia to see the different colours and shapes of petals. What could they all do in this room to make time pass now? She would be content to sit and read Tanizaki, but she knew Chris would feel restless and fidgety now that the present seemed like a repeat of the past. While she appreciated nothingness as a destination, he would want to fill up the time.

Chris asked Mia if she wanted to read some more. He raised one of the books he had brought from home, curious if she wanted the story about Eva, a girl with a unicorn.

'Yes, but I need to pee first,' Mia said. Tarisa wondered how long Mia had been needing to pee, whether she needed to be rushed to the bathroom or if they could slowly make their way there.

'When was the last time she peed?' Tarisa asked Chris.

He hesitated. 'I don't remember.'

This answer annoyed her, but she turned away to hide it.

It wasn't clear which of them Mia was talking to, or if she had meant to be ambiguous. Tarisa hesitated.

'I'll take her,' Tarisa said.

'Oh, you sure? I can take her.'

'No, it's okay. Get some rest. I'll be gone for the evening, so you do your thing now.'

'Oh, okay, thanks. What time's that class again?'

'At five, in about three hours. Then I've got that Gina Vahlen show afterwards.' She had bought tickets for this Franco-Austrian choreographer's show a few weeks ago, planning to go alone, even though she had a few friends from dance classes. She disliked the back-and-forth in coordinating to make dates and times work for everyone, a process that must always happen in parallel with other theatregoers threatening to consume the seats she desired. Then, there was also the anxiety of losing that seat per se, an anxiety that she wanted to avoid, and knew she could avoid by planning as a loner from the beginning.

'Do you prefer I take a cab so I can stay here with you longer?' she asked Chris.

'Oh, no, no. No need. Please, just take the bus if you want to.'

'Are you sure?'

'Yes.'

'Are you sure-sure?'

'Yes, I'm sure-sure.'

'Why don't we have a car?' Mia interrupted.

'It's Singapore. We live downtown. There are buses, trains, taxis, shared rides all over.' Tarisa explained.

'Why do my friends have cars?'

'Because they have siblings, and their parents can't cart them all around on taxis and buses. It's too much work.'

'I'm not too much work?' Mia asked.

'Well, you are, but it's still better than paying so much money for a car here. It's the most expensive country in the world to own a car, Mia,' Tarisa said.

'But we're rich,' Mia said.

'What?' Tarisa said. She looked at Chris, who seemed equally stunned.

'I said, "but we're rich",' Mia pulled her head back and looked at them blankly.

'Where'd you get that from, Mia?' Tarisa asked.

'I'm not sure,' she said.

Tarisa looked at Chris for him to explain their finances to Mia. That Mia had to pee seemed forgotten by all.

'We're not rich, Mia,' Chris said.

Tarisa rolled her eyes at him playfully. They had both agreed that they would never give Mia the details of Chris' family's wealth. They had always just said, 'We are more privileged than other people.'

'We are more privileged than other people,' Tarisa said now. 'But we also must be sensible about how we use money.'

'What does that mean?' Mia asked.

'It means that just because we have money, we don't use as much of it as we want. We need to save too. You never know when money will just disappear,' Tarisa said.

'How could money just disappear?'

'If you overspend, for example,' Chris said.

'Or if your dad loses his job and we need to live off savings. In that case, there'd be no new money coming in. We'd have to use up what we have, with no new money coming in.'

'Why will Daddy lose his job?'

'It's just hypothetical, Mia,' Tarisa said. 'I mean it's something that could happen. To anyone. People get thrown off their plans all the time.'

'That's why we don't just buy a car in Singapore,' Chris said.

'Or take a taxi. We also take the bus, right?' Tarisa added.

'Well, actually,' Chris said with a chuckle, 'You could take a taxi, T. You could always take a taxi.'

'Is a Grab a taxi?' Mia asked.

'No, it's a shared ride: private cars that act similarly to taxis. It's part of innovation, people changing things up all the time,' Tarisa said. She suddenly remembered Mia's pee. 'But they're still more expensive than buses, so I like to take the bus.' Tarisa slid her hands under Mia's armpits to lift her off the cot.

'I'd never taken so many buses until I met you,' Chris said, sliding onto the daybed with a copy of the most recent *The New Yorker*. From the warmth of his voice, she could tell that he was satisfied, even amused, speaking about his own change.

'You haven't peed in your pants yet, right?' Tarisa asked Mia.

'Not yet.'

'Let's go pee,' Tarisa said.

She closed the bathroom door in case a nurse would suddenly barge in. Tarisa lifted Mia up onto the toilet bowl and held her underarms to support her weight.

'Come, grip onto my shoulders,' she said, pulling Mia towards her.

'Nothing.'

'Nothing? But you said you needed to pee.'

'I know, but now there's nothing.'

Tarisa began to tickle Mia's tummy. A year ago, during the ordeal of potty-training, a period which saw puddles and wet footprints around the apartment, she had read that tickling children's tummies helped their bladder to release. 'You can do it,' she whispered now.

Mia leaned in, as usual, her head almost over her mother's shoulders.

'Tickle, tickle, *whee!*' Tarisa sounded joyful.

Mia peed as if a waterfall were exiting her body. Tarisa wondered if it wasn't a sign of growth that Mia could wait to use the bathroom. *That would be nice. Growth would be nice.*

There was so much pee that Tarisa had to use more toilet paper than usual to wipe Mia's thighs where urine had splattered. She suddenly remembered Leela's words and expectations, that one day Tarisa would help wash *her* pee off her legs when Tarisa's filial piety met with Leela's old age. Then, the thought came that one day Mia might be the one to do this for her. She wouldn't ask for it, the transmission of filial piety being something of a question for herself, but Mia generally seemed sweet and kind, the kind of person whose future held wiping her mother's wet legs.

'Time to wash our hands,' Tarisa said, almost singing. She helped Mia off the seat and helped her onto the stool, standing behind her. She found joy helping rub soap onto the small knobs of fat beside Mia's knuckles, their fingers big and small collaborating. There was an intimacy in the act that Tarisa cherished—the mother's chasing after spots yet uncovered, a promise of protection drafted as a practice of hygiene.

'What do we do now, Mommy?' Mia asked as Tarisa unlocked the door.

'Now I google my bus route to the studio,' she said.

'Can we play?'

'Play what, sweetie?'

They stepped out.

'Something.'

Tarisa walked after Mia onto the cot, dreading the pretend-play that might be coming up, and picked up her phone. She tapped the studio name into Google Maps. 'What kind of something?' she asked Mia. 'Twenty-eight, so thirty, minutes,' she mumbled to herself, then looked at Chris, who was on the couch, checking for his mood. *Seems fine.*

'Let's play "family",' Mia said.

'We *are* family,' Tarisa replied, hoping to change Mia's mind.

'No, but let's *play* family. Like you be the big sister and I'm the little sister and Daddy be the small brother.'

'Can we do something else?' Tarisa grunted.

'No!'

'Yes!' she retorted playfully.

'No!'

'I can leave at four-fifteen to be safe?' Tarisa changed the subject, looking at Chris.

'Even earlier if you want,' he said.

'No, it's fine. Four-fifteen's cool.'

'Okay, but don't worry about us, yeah? I mean, they're taking good care of her.'

'It's good we have them here.'

'Mommy, please, family!' Mia interrupted.

'Yeah,' Chris said at the same time.

'One sec, Mia,' Tarisa answered. 'When's that IV drip coming?' She wondered if she'd have to be here to listen to Mia's torment when the needle went in.

'Soon,' Chris said.

'Mommy,' Mia interrupted again. 'I said let's play family!'

'Oh, sweetheart! Your request is bizarre! It's like if I proposed to your father, "Hey, Chris, let's play Husband and Wife"!'

She knew that the equivalence she had made was somewhat flawed. And yet, as soon as she finished the sentence, she could not help thinking: *When was the last time Chris and I played Husband and Wife?* The way Tanizaki put it in *A Companion*, that relationship was defined by whether the two people had sex. Even if they got along well and liked each other indiscriminately, what affirmed their status as husband or wife was the presence or absence of reciprocated lust. Tarisa questioned this definition, but she also wondered if it was because she had to, to preserve the legitimacy of her marriage in her mind. It was a terrifying thought that her marriage no longer existed, that all she had with this man was a label—like a roof under which there was no home.

She didn't know if she and Chris were *really* husband and wife if they didn't, and couldn't, have sex. But many people, she knew, also had sexless marriages—it was a subject on the internet—and she wouldn't say *their* marriages were invalid. As she visited this thought—it was not the first time—a brief knock interrupted her. She moved away from the idea—in her mind, she saw it fall off, crashing onto the ground, breaking and shooting out debris.

'Hello! Doctor said add IV drip,' Gracie said, barging in. Her long brisk steps signalled that she was used to entering other people's spaces this way. Geetha and Mui followed suit.

'Oh, we were just talking about it,' Tarisa said. She wanted to smile at Gracie, and a smile did come out, but it was less genuine than the one she'd given Gracie before she had lied and told Mia that she would be going home.

Gracie pouted. 'IV drip for her medicine, because girl-girl not drinking medicine properly,' she said.

'Could you please wait a second? I was just taking her to the bathroom,' Tarisa lied, holding onto Mia's shoulders. She shot Chris a look to quickly let him know that she was up to something. 'Could you just wait until we come out, Nurse Gracie?'

'Sure ma'am.'

'Thank you.' She took Mia by her underarms and lifted her off the bed. When Mia's feet settled into the floor, Tarisa touched her shoulder lightly and began running her hand down her arm, which provoked Mia to instinctively raise her hand up to hold her mother's. Skin-to-skin, they walked towards the blue cornflower tiles.

Tarisa locked the bathroom door. An instinct had guided her to do so.

'Mom, what she say?' Mia asked. They were standing in the shower area, as far from the door as possible. Their feet were in the pools of water Chris' showering had left behind.

'She said you need to have an IV drip,' Tarisa whispered.

'What is that?' Mia echoed her volume.

'It's the thing you had last year, where they put medicine in through your hand.'

Mia launched into a cry immediately.

'It's okay, Mia. It's medicine that you don't have to take with your mouth, okay?'

Mia sobbed harder.

'But I don't like medicine!'

'Mia, they think you're peeing. Don't cry. You wouldn't cry if you were really peeing. Listen,' Tarisa continued to whisper, but making sure to hold a steady gaze with Mia now. She cradled Mia's hands in hers. 'This is drip medicine. It's not like normal medicine. You won't even feel it. It goes in you directly without you having to open your mouth. Okay?'

'Can I have the one that goes in my bum-bum?' Her volume had come down.

'The suppository? You're too big for that now.'

'I want the one that goes in my bum-bum!' Her volume had increased again.

'Mia, you're too big for that now.'

'I don't want medicine!'

'You'll be fine,' Tarisa said, moving one hand to stroke her back. 'I came in here to let you know that we won't be going home right after this. No matter what Nurse Gracie says. And you will be fine. Daddy and I are here with you.'

'But you go dance.'

'I'll come back after I dance.'

Mia cried more. Tarisa could see her saliva beginning to grow into long lines between her teeth.

'Sweetheart, stop. It's gonna be okay, Mia.'

'I don't want medicine!'

'Shh! Mia, Mia. It's okay. It will make the monsters in your body go away more quickly.'

'Mom, I don't want medicine!'

'It's okay. It's okay. It'll be fast, okay? And then you'll have a really cool machine on you that makes you look like a cute little robot.' Tarisa swung her arms around robotically. 'Come on, the nurses are waiting.'

'Mommy.'

'Mia, we can't live in the bathroom forever. There's no food in the bathroom. No air in the bathroom. I'm right here, Mia. I'm right here.'

'You'll need to leave because we need a sterile environment again, Ma'am, Sir,' Geetha said as soon as Tarisa opened the door and met her gaze. She hadn't waited even slightly to say this.

Outside, Chris and Tarisa listened to Mia's distress. Her cries were nothing new, and nothing that made them want to swing open the door to save her. This, too, would pass.

'Would have been easier for her to take the medicine at home,' Chris said.

Who is a man who stands beside you at a hospital, concerned about the same child? Mia's father. Mia's something. What, though, is he in relation to me?

Tarisa saw him in her peripheral vision. She could not make out who he was to her, what the distance between them meant.

CHAPTER 16

Mia looked different, puffy eyes and a red nose accentuating her face. A clumsy machine towered over her. A thick board stuck to her lower right arm.

'What's this for?' Tarisa asked, pointing to the board. She could not remember what it did.

'To immobilize, Mommy. So, she cannot break the needle when she moves around,' Mui replied.

Tarisa looked at Mia, no longer free to roam. 'Wow! Nice accessory, Mia!' she said, pretending to be enthusiastic despite wondering how the child felt now. The nurses' smiles widened when they heard this. Bidding a quick goodbye, they cruised out.

Mia opened her arms, begging for a hug, which Tarisa gave her readily. Chris swooped in too and kissed the crown of her head.

'You did a good job, Mia. This is for medicine. Your little body needs it right now, okay?' Tarisa said.

Mia continued to bawl, each second that her voice boomed triggered Tarisa to hug her more tightly.

'Good job, sweetie,' Tarisa said. She took the tube connected to the machine in her fingers.

'You see this little drip-drip right here?' She pointed with another hand and made her voice higher, more captivating. Mia stopped crying and followed her mother's finger, travelling down the tube. 'It's going right into your body.' Tarisa began to swish her fingertip in zigzags on Mia's chest down to her tummy and then swirled and swirled it around Mia's navel. 'And it's gonna go right in and right in and zap and kill all the monsters in your body.'

'Really?'

'Yes, that's why it's necessary.'

'Mommy.'

'Yes?'

'I need to pee.'

'Again? But you just did.'

'You tickled me.'

'I didn't tickle you. I swished my finger.'

'It was like tickle.'

In the bathroom, as Mia's eyeline rested in her mother's, Tarisa heard water trickling down the toilet. It was a sound she had come to associate with closeness and ephemerality. The day this human became conscious of its own growing, it would want privacy, to stop having a mother intently watch it emptying its bladder. This sound, of a door in Mia's body opening and releasing liquid, was a sound within a timeframe, of innocence that bred dependence, of dependence that gave a chance to bond and to trust. Each time Mia locked eyes with Tarisa while seated on the toilet bowl, Tarisa remembered that the child was not yet an entire product of social conventions; she was still a raw fledgling who used even urination as a process to seek help and stare into the eyes of the helper.

'Are you done, sweetie? Lemme wipe you, okay?'

'I do my own, Mommy. Why so much pee?'

'Because the doctor said to stuff as much water into your body as we can. Has Daddy been trying to make you drink? Did you drink a lot of water when I was at the library?'

'Yes.'

'That's why.'

'Mommy, I do my own.'

'No, sweetheart. Lemme help you now, okay?'

'No, Mommy, I do my own!'

She thought about the pee that would get on Mia's hands, Mia touching the tap with that hand, then Tarisa herself having to scrub the tap after sending Mia out of the bathroom. Tarisa sighed. She took a deep breath to calm down. It all would have been easier if she could clean Mia herself.

But I should reward her for getting the IV drip. I should surrender.

'Okay, sweetheart. Just, just try to keep your hands as clean as possible, okay? While still getting the pee. Whatever pee's left on your vagina.' She always said 'vagina' knowing it was weird. She'd never had to refer to a vagina like this in any other context.

'Okay, Mommy.'

'But, see, you can use only your left hand. Your right hand is stuck to this thing.' She shook the pole ever so gently.

'It's okay, Mommy. I can use my left hand.'

'Hmm.' Tarisa held her words in. When Mia was done, her wet hand splotchy and streaked with urine, Tarisa took a deep inhale and guided her to the sink, holding Mia's arm up and tugging the machine pole behind her to leave enough space between the child and the pole in case she should suddenly pivot around. 'Sweetheart, you have one hand left. Your other hand is bandaged and stuck to a board. You need me to help you wash, all right?'

'Why they stuck my hand to a board?'

'To stop your hand from moving here and there, they said.' Tarisa ran the water and lifted Mia's left hand into the sink.

'Why?'

Tarisa added the soap. 'Because it would be dangerous for you to have a needle inside you and move here and there.'

'Why?'

'Because the needle might break inside you.'

'What happens if the needle breaks inside me?'

'You'll probably have an ouchie.'

'Big ouchie?'

'Yeah. I mean, I don't know if you'd *die*, but you'd probably have an ouchie, because something just broke inside your vessels, and it's not supposed to.' Tarisa didn't like herself for explaining this to Mia so matter-of-factly. She felt she had failed in her goal of keeping her away from the word 'die'. She thought that Chris, who was constantly afraid of family members dying because of his father's near-death incident, had already been talking about death too regularly. 'Don't do that, Mia. It will make you die,' he had often said, in different contexts. He didn't let her go on boats, budget airlines, or taxis, even on short trips on local roads, if they hadn't brought a car seat along. Tarisa felt she needed to compensate for how much he threw the idea of death at Mia. But now, she had messed up by mentioning death to her again. Luckily, Mia didn't seem to sense any oddness in her death being referenced once more. Tarisa washed off the last bits of soap, gliding her fingers over Mia's hand to make sure there weren't any soapy areas left. 'Okay, done. Let's go, sweetie,' she said, the sweetness and the intimacy of washing her hands still feeling the same as the last time, even with only one side left.

She waited for Mia to begin moving first, so that she could manoeuvre the machine according to her path and prevent her from falling.

CHAPTER 17

'Goodnight in advance,' Tarisa had said to them both before heading out to the dance studio.

She saw the café in the garden, with young families slowly trickling out and children refusing to leave bouncy castles. Tarisa had never thought to bring Mia here. Even exciting bouncy castles wouldn't save her from Mia's clutch. Mia wouldn't go into a bouncy castle alone. She would want Mommy or Daddy to go in and jump with her too, instead of letting them watch her from the comfort of a table.

Tarisa expected to be back after ten. She knew Chris would have food to eat. She had pre-ordered fish porridge from dining services. She remembered that it tasted decent. She knew that Chris would pick the fish out, eat it, and leave the rice untouched. He thought that the hospital's rice was mediocre, and he believed that mediocre rice wasn't worth his stomach space. Rich Thai people could be picky about the quality of their rice. She remembered when she was a child, when her family could go to a nice restaurant, her mother would comment on the fragrance of the rice. Leela would purse her lips and shake her head slowly, moaning while her mouth was full, as if in paradise. It was the same kind of rice that Chris' family ate every day, their normal.

When Tarisa arrived at the studio, only Edwina was there. She smiled copiously—the way Tarisa used to when she was twenty-two—and came over to hug her. Tarisa felt enveloped by her muscles and strength. Her black-diamond hair fell over Tarisa's shoulders, smooth and soothing, curtaining Tarisa off from wherever she had just arrived from.

Ever since Mia had settled into school, Tarisa had had time to revisit her childhood hobby of dance. Once a week, for almost eight months now. The classes were pretty regular: even if Mia was sick, Chris would be home to take care of her and let Tarisa off for her classes.

This evening, Edwina was doing a movement therapy special, something that Tarisa had never done, and that Edwina had told her was a pilot for what she planned to teach for the rest of her life. Edwina was twenty-two, and Tarisa was glad that a person of that age had already found her raison d'être. That said, Edwina had also just married and said that a child was in the plans for the following year or the year after. Tarisa found herself wondering what impact that would have on Edwina's plans. She never told her that it was something she sometimes considered.

The door swung open, and another familiar figure came in. 'Oh, hello! What brings *you* here?' Tarisa tried to hide her curiosity as a casual greeting, although if Mei Ching had answered, she would have felt pleased to know why someone else might have come to a movement therapy class as well.

'Wassup?' Mei Ching answered, giving Tarisa her knuckles for a bump, then running her hand through her new pixie cut.

Edwina gave Mei Ching the same powerful hug and excused herself to go prepare the playlist.

'What's up? I didn't know you were coming,' Tarisa tried to prod a little. Nobody else in her circles talked about their problems. In dance classes, people came, danced, and left. In conversations at school, other mothers kept conversations at a superficial level.

'Yeah, you too!' Mei Ching answered, while pulling off her sweatpants and looking at her bruised legs.

'I was curious about what this movement therapy thing was all about, so I came,' Tarisa said, looking away from the bruise, not wanting to seem like she was prying, though she kept it in her peripheral vision.

'Yeah, me, too,' Mei Ching continued, seeming to not think twice about her bruise. 'Hey, you were a writer, right?'

Tarisa was about to refute, *Well, a food writer, and then a waitress, and most recently, a researcher writing academic papers.*

'Let me give you something I just published.' Mei Ching opened her tote bag and handed Tarisa a booklet that had been stapled together. The staples were lopsided. 'Poems I wrote.'

Tarisa took it and felt its lightness. 'Thanks. Poems.' She flipped through the pages. She noticed all the pronouns referring to the speaker were 'his,' 'him,' or 'he.' She understood immediately that she wasn't the only one in the room who pondered over her identity.

In addition to Mei Ching, there were Paulina and Maya. They were quieter people Tarisa had seen a few times in dance classes. Tarisa didn't ask why they had showed up today. However, she tried to guess from their movements what was on their minds. Paulina always seemed focused on slithering and moving her shoulders in circles, backwards more often than forwards, keeping her eyes closed. Maya, always quick to remember a new dance, kept her eyes open and ploughed through the choreography as if reciting vocabulary for a test.

This was the group with whom Tarisa felt most comfortable, bodies being employed as bodies, no roles attached. For the next two hours, they would be limbs, muscles contorted in whatever shape Edwina prompted them into, but there would never be a role. They would just be masses provoked.

Edwina pulled the curtains over the mirror. 'Now you cannot see yourselves. Focus on your interiority. The point is to open your mind to become more relaxed, through noticing and taking advantage of everything in the environment. If you came late, notice how that makes your body feel. Are there areas where it is tenser? Are there areas where it feels giddier? Are there areas that feel particularly apologetic? Like a rush of *buzzzzzz* that sounds like your body just wants to scream and cry? *Why*,' Edwina said immediately, then left her voice hanging for a second before picking it up again, 'were you late? Were you trying to finish up something at work? Were you late in catching the bus? Were you, I don't know, doing laundry?'

Edwina cruised around as she asked these questions and invited them to begin to move in any way that made them comfortable and more relaxed. Tarisa closed her eyes and felt her movement, every limb rising and lowering like water adjusting to a riverbend.

Tarisa heard two claps. She turned. Edwina was walking away from the corner and coming into the centre of the spacious studio to gather them. 'Come in, come in!' she said with a smile, waving for them to make the circle of their bodies even tighter. 'Wait, we don't have to stand in a circle!'

They tried to stack themselves into a more staggered, loose group. Tarisa felt, already, the discomfort of deciding where she should establish herself in the group. She moved forward by an inch or two, hoping that the others would do the hard work of deciding exactly how they would fit together. Shyly, they did, looking at their shuffling feet, as if by avoiding eye contact, they would assume less responsibility for the choices they made.

'Hey.'
'Hey.'
'Hey.'
'Hey.'

They all said to one another when they looked up.

'Separate yourselves a bit,' Edwina said. 'For the next few minutes, I want you to continue listening to my prompt and just let your body react. You can close your eyes or open them, whatever you want. I want you to feel how your fingers are moving, how your limbs are moving, if there's a little space in between each finger or each limb where you can move some more.'

For the first time, Tarisa's mind was clear enough to notice the room. A black box, like they were in an unlit phone screen.

Tarisa awaited Edwina's directions, not caring what they would be. She just wanted to hear the prompts, which would direct and liberate her at once. Edwina did not know what Tarisa's past twelve hours had involved—that about twelve hours ago, she was getting out of a taxi and walking into a hospital lobby, that she was only awake because of hospital coffee, that she had slept in a cot, that she would be going back and sleeping in it again tonight after a show.

'Has everyone found a position they're comfortable in?' Edwina asked, smiling, showing her teeth. They nodded or smiled back. 'First,' Edwina's voice eased into a smooth flow, 'I want you to pretend,' she inhaled, 'your feet are in a pot of honey.' She released a breath with the word 'honey'. Tarisa could hear her exhale conjuring the softness of the liquid. 'You can choose if you want to close your eyes or open your eyes. It's up to you.' Edwina closed her eyes. 'I want you to focus on your feet. How are they registering the presence of the honey? How would they move? What kind of resistance? What dynamics?' Tarisa noted Edwina's pattern: stringing together three or four questions, then dropping them into complete silence—there was no music—so that the ideas could be absorbed into their bodies.

The prompt changed her existence in the room. Not yet moving, Tarisa felt the stickiness of her feet on the parquet floor. She felt her stiff, erect body sway slightly forward and then back, balancing more energy than she had expected. She let it pendulate gently back and forth and left and right. It was there that she began to think that it was a pool of warm, golden honey moving, applying pressure that pushed her in different directions. For a brief second, she imagined that she was in a place as dazzlingly golden as Aladdin's Cave of Wonders, but her own obedience stopped her. *That wasn't the prompt, the prompt was feet. Feet only, in pot.* She scaled down the honey and let it crawl only up to her ankles. She imagined a pot, one that looked a lot like Winnie the Pooh's. She allowed her feet to splay apart in an imperfect first position, then let her neck drop forward; it chose to hang to the left. She tried to drain her control from her arms and fingers.

Her toes wiggled first. She raised both heels up slowly, focusing on balancing, trying not to wobble and tip the pot over. She imagined the curtain of honey stretching from her heel to the pot, and she gave it time to slide into a thick V and drip as a single strand from each heel. There was pleasure in the wait.

She started to lower both heels, and once they were close to the floor, she circled her neck to the left and rolled her shoulders back and turned out her knees in a gentle plié. Her right shoulder dropped. Her left shoulder rose. Her left heel surged upward again, bringing with it another strand of honey, which she gently squished again when she brought the heel to the ground.

'And your ankles?' Edwina asked.

Keeping her feet down, Tarisa pivoted her left ankle outward, letting her heel slide ahead of her toes. She tried to hold both feet tightly to the ground to experience the resistance of the honey. The right foot gave way to a desire, from somewhere, to invert and pull back. Both sets of toes now found themselves opposite each other. She allowed her right foot some authority and a more active role, acknowledging that she had neglected it so far. She glided her right toes back inward, trying to tug her right ankle away from the pool of honey.

'Now, the honey is deeper, up to your knees. How would you move? How would you get around?' Edwina asked.

Tarisa tried to lift her right leg, meeting resistance in the air. She held her balance firmly on her left leg, while she brought her right shin up, letting her right knee escape the pool of honey, and tried to swirl her foot around in a honey-doused circle, feeling the decadence of the honey's thickness.

'And your knees. How would they move?' Edwina asked.

Tarisa kept her right foot lifted and manoeuvred it behind her. She was losing balance and opened her eyes. She lifted the foot up higher than her knee and let the honey trickle down her calf. She felt it slowly drizzle down: warm, smooth gold liquid, dripping from her feet, moving over from her lower calf, and coating the seams of her leggings, which seemed to no longer exist, because she felt the honey on her knee. She swirled her knee around, and before she could finish the third swirl, lowered the knee slightly, letting her leg return to the pool of liquid, extending her leg into a low développé to resist the honey's encroaching pressure. She bent her left knee slightly and released her neck to the right, letting it hang briefly, then pulled her right leg up again, feeling her foot hang. The honey droplets from her toes returned to the honey pool. She was deep in, but unafraid. She was certain that she could overcome it.

'Don't forget that you also have your top body!' Edwina teased. 'Everything that happens is part of a flow.'

Tarisa continued to move, her body interacting with itself, taking commands under her skin in places she couldn't see.

Edwina never asked them to imagine the honey all the way up over their heads. She never asked them to imagine suffocating.

'Slowly, slowly, now, open your eyes.'

In the mirror, Tarisa met herself. A young mother. A mother with a body so small and lean that it amazed people to learn that she was really a mother. She saw a woman who had it together, a woman whose body was the envy of countless women, a woman whose husband was the dream of countless women, a woman whose child was the dream of countless women, a woman who danced, undeterred, on an evening her child was in a hospital ward.

'How'd that feel?' Edwina asked, sweeping her hair with her hands and beaming at them.

Tarisa felt light, like there were no more edges in her body. She felt like one of the cargo ships that glided serenely past her apartment window, with her head as the control room. Those ships, she remembered now, moved so imperceptibly. Whenever an eagle came, swirling around the sky, fifty floors high, the scene came out of its still-life frame. *Like me now.*

Giant toys in a billionaire's bathtub. Buoyant ships, though made of steel.

Limb after limb, Tarisa concentrated on the places in her body where she had crushed away the knots. She had felt so much bone in her body in the past few years. The hardness of the bones, their inflexible edges, had taken up so much of her movement, and now between them, there was more air.

Outside, in front of the studio door, where Tarisa was transitioning into the world outside, she said, 'So good,' to Mei Ching, who cocked her chin up again and said, 'Yeah.' Paulina and Maya smiled, waved, and said, 'See you again.'

Tarisa watched the two women get into their street shoes and say goodbye to each other, heading to staircases at opposite sides of the corridor. On the ground floor, one would likely end up trailing just behind the other. *They could have just gone down together. Why did they scatter as soon as possible?*

They never got together after the workshop to hang out, which is why Tarisa never knew more about them, including their reason for attending the classes.

'Do you want to grab dinner?' Mei Ching surprisingly asked.

'I'd love to but—' Tarisa regretted now that she would miss this chance to connect—'I have a dance show. Gina Vahlen's. Any chance you're going too?' She had sometimes run into Mei Ching at dance events, there also alone.

'Not this time. I'm trying to save up. Wanna quit my job.' Although Tarisa had never seen makeup on Mei Ching's face, she worked at a cosmetics company where the people were 'toxic'. She said she needed the money.

'Maybe I can still walk with you for now.' Excited about connections that might be in the making now, Tarisa popped into the studio once more. 'Edwina, would you like to walk down together?' She thought about a pack growing, a community bound by the desire to move by prompts to enter a rare state of self-knowledge.

'I have to do emails,' Edwina said, glowing.

A dancer who has to 'do emails'. Admin is in every life.

Tarisa took what she could of Edwina's glow and her smile that seemed so at home on her face, remembering how happiness looked at Edwina's stage of life.

Mei Ching scampered down the steps. Tinier and bonier than Tarisa, she could pass for a thirteen-year-old. (She was really twenty-three.) Her body took up so little space that it made Tarisa think about her body just flying away and disappearing. She imagined holding onto Mei Ching's legs and asking Mei Ching to float towards the sky.

On the ground floor, they walked past the last of the families in the café. Parents whose eyes still hid behind sunglasses finished the last few sips of what was left, diluted by ice. Sunshine was no longer as threatening. Children jumped on the bouncy castle, whose plastic skin must have felt cooler now. A toddler kicked a ball in Tarisa's direction and looked in awe as her foot caught it. She smiled and gently kicked it back. Mia came to her mind.

There were pools of sweat attached to Tarisa's back. She wanted to change out of her clothes, but she didn't want to ruin the momentum of walking with Mei Ching.

'So how was that session for you?' Tarisa asked.

'Good. Really good,' Mei Ching said right away without elaboration.

Tarisa didn't press further. She had learned that most people outside of America were not as chatty as Americans, and that sometimes silence was, for both parties, a more comfortable instrument to create a bond. It had taken her more than a year to get used to the quietness as she tried to make local friends. (Yet, in the end, she felt that silence had given her more acquaintances than friends.) She had started to consider that she didn't need to care so much about having friends because she had a family. The people who didn't seem interested in making friends were the ones with families, so maybe she should figure out how to make family feel enough for herself too.

But she would love it if Mei Ching shared more.

'I think moving and being in touch with my body is really helping me to get over what happened. When that woman touched me,' Mei Ching continued.

Tarisa remembered Mei Ching's bruise.

'I don't know,' Mei Ching said. She sounded like there was a reel playing in her mind. 'I'm still trying to get over it.'

Tarisa nodded. She was getting what she wanted, but it felt risky, perhaps even cruel, to ask for more. She didn't want to scare Mei Ching away, and she questioned whether she wasn't even sick for using someone else's abuse as a way to connect.

'Did *you* find that helpful?' Mei Ching asked. The deflection set Tarisa aback. She wondered if she had appeared disinterested. Maybe Mei Ching had been extending an overture and seeing if Tarisa was interested in her story. She should have asked questions. She had let the chance for a connection slip.

'Yeah, definitely.' *I missed the chance.* 'I feel,' she started, though as she ran through her vocabulary, all of it seemed inept. 'I feel good.' *I missed the chance. Let's not talk about me. Let's talk about you.*

'Damn, right!' Mei Ching nearly shouted, snapping her fingers. 'Anyway, lemme know what you think of the poems I wrote,' she said, darting off to the crosswalk for the bus stop.

Stop. Don't go.

Tarisa watched as Mei Ching's backpack slapped her bony spine as she ran across. She imagined Mei Ching slipping in and out of places quickly and undetected because she was so small. Today Mei Ching had slipped away, after so kindly giving her a chance.

***

At Victoria Theatre, Tarisa followed the thin crowd into the black box. She recognized nobody. Everyone was a stranger. She found her seat among the rows of red chairs in the centre. It was small and hard, and forced her to sit up tall. When she did, she saw dirt covering the stage, uneven mounds of fuzzy-looking brown that hinted at the setting being outdoors.

An usher handed her a brochure, giving Tarisa information she hadn't earlier known. She had not looked into details before coming. The ticket that she held was not an expression of interest in the story as much as an imprecise desire to see something new.

> *Assembly* takes place at a party—it portrays the rising and falling of emotions. The audience's physical experience and the state of being of the performer are main concerns. Fifteen dancers organize themselves into varying degrees of intimacy, as each relates to individual and collective emotions displayed by the group. The community that results gravitates towards irretrievably heightened emotional intensity.

Words stuck out—intimacy, collective emotions—rippling through her without conjuring a specific beginning or ending image.

In the background, she heard people talking about their friendships and romances. Their voices came in waves. She listened, closing her eyes.

At these sounds of relationships and communities, her mind began to travel away from Victoria Theatre. She pictured her last office, where she wrote papers. As life would have it, just as her first trimester was ending, Tarisa's old professors in Boston had written to ask if she wanted to do research at a foundation of their recent affiliation, and she had agreed to it, finding it as close as she could get to getting that PhD that she had, by now, foregone. There was no such person there yet as a Mr Ooi. Tarisa's pregnancy had been advancing smoothly, she did not think parenthood would be more difficult, and she did not envision herself being anything but a working mother, especially when she could work from home.

Chris had agreed that she should take the opportunity her professors were presenting. After all, finding a job as a foreigner in Singapore beyond the domains of finance or scientific research contained an impossible reach. This might be the one chance for her to escape the situation that she was beginning to find herself in: pregnant and not much else.

Chris' support had come with no conditions. How he talked about her career now, clear of obstruction, differed from how he had talked about it in October. *He knows that he owes me.* Sitting together on the couch, lumped in one corner though there was plenty of space for two, they had agreed that she would do her best in the interview—everything about the baby, they would play by ear. Whatever the future needed, this job opportunity now took priority.

Tarisa imagined this as a chance to crawl out of the chasm of women's online pleas. In closed forums, boxes of text—some typed most eruditely—neighboured painted, glamorous faces whose symmetry never betrayed imperfection. A pattern of women wanting to work surfaced, detailing how long a family had been in Singapore, how old their children had become, what leads they had desperately followed, and their aches and pains as they craned their necks to sniff the air for this thing that their husbands had come to Singapore with and had never been without: a career. They thought they, too, would have one. No one had said giving it up for the men would be a thing of forever.

'But what was it, to be fed in a golden cage?' one woman had asked.

'We must still be grateful,' one replied.

'We must continue to try,' another wrote.

Tarisa went to a casual interview over lunch with an American, David, who ordered only orange juice and broth, so she, despite being pregnant and hungry, ordered just a few mushroom dumplings. She did not say anything about a looming baby, grateful for the fact that her shirt still fell flat tucked into her pencil skirt. When she did mention it two weeks later, David, noticing her copious yawning on her way into a rare meeting that forced her to miss a nap, lunged towards her with a hug, saying he would find her a room to 'pump and do all that' if she needed one. He went to his office, the one with the mahogany desk that Mr Ooi would eventually sit behind, returning with a bottle from his juice-detox supply. He offered it to her, and she took it, watching the juice shake gently as it changed hands.

On a day when Tarisa's belly was big, David was suddenly gone. Tarisa heard from her colleagues that they, the men on the board who never came down into the office, thought his policies towards his staff were too lenient. The board, made of people who were closer to natural death than birth, put an old-school man in David's place. Mr Ooi, who asked work-from-home to change to office-hours, signalled at the first staff meeting, leaning in when he spoke, drawing out when others did, that he had no intention to renew contracts of mothers. He did not say it directly. Instead, he looked at every woman in the office as he said this: 'Some people, uh, when they have children, can no longer commit to work, and if you can't commit to work, it's difficult to have you in a team.'

Tilting her head back into the Victoria Theatre seat now, she thought about the ordinariness of everything preceding those words. *It was a fine, productive day. We were writing on white boards. I was doing a good job—and then. And then we had a staff meeting.*

The theatre lights dimmed, and she tried to think about something else. The new darkness made her think about dark mornings in Bangkok, which she had experienced as a child. She used to walk to bus stops before sunrise with her mother, at 5 a.m., the irony being that this was her mode of transportation to get to an expensive international school. Most students were driven by uniformed chauffeurs in their parents' luxury sedans or took the school bus, but even the latter was too expensive for her family. Her father's income as a diplomat was not a lot, and she was able to attend this school only because of subsidies.

Tarisa's young hands would come together on the bus, which was notorious for speeding. She would pray for the bus to not crash.

Any bus that she took now was a choice. Buses in Singapore felt safe, a way to stay grounded.

The music for the show began. It was techno, the kind of sound that could accompany her fears on her childhood rides.

Tarisa glanced at her left wrist to see what time it was, trying to estimate when the show might end. Instead of a watch, she saw that she had a hospital wristband. It said that her name was Mia, that her surname was Chris', and that she was three years old. She realized that she was likely the only one in the theatre with a hospital wristband, and though the situation might have seemed absurd—*A mother here while her child is hospitalized!*—she remained confident in choosing to be present. She would have gone to a raucous, rowdy, shimmery show at Marina Bay Sands, smiled, and laughed with unrelenting bright lights and gaudy showmen if that was what she had booked. She looked on her other wrist, where the watch was. She had never had a hard and fast rule about which side to put it on. It was almost 9 p.m., and she imagined Chris and Mia were already asleep. She forgot about the speeding bus. The dancers appeared.

A woman's body began to drift across. The hood of her jacket—bright yellow and blue, popping out amid the darkness of the rest of the stage—covered her head. She glided slowly across, travelling in slow-motion as her feet journeyed across invisible bridges in the air each time she made a step, resisting the music's ravishing, dogged beats.

Tarisa could not ignore the music. She couldn't tell what this track said or how it would end and escape from its own loop. Nothing in the music was predictable—new sounds entered as they wished, swimming on top of old beats, until the song encased elements that battled within its abyss. A warping noise sometimes sucked them all out, before they would bounce back in, cannibalizing the music again.

The hooded dancer walked downstage. One by one, others entered from the side, a crowd slowly fomenting on the dirt. Loudness arrived on stage without them saying anything or the music increasing in volume.

Tarisa's attention was drawn towards one of the new dancers: a tall young woman with a bob unfavourable to her. Tight jeans and a T-shirt covered up parts of her body but left her torso out and open. Muscles cut beautifully onto the skin around her navel.

A grin painted her face, where one might see a door if one imagined her head as a home a child might draw, with a triangular, slanted roof, and a door in the middle of the wall.

Behind that mouth, she wanted something badly. She reached out to a man and tried to pull him close against her. Their skin collided. In the slow-motion in which they were roving, what would have been a brief stamp of violence in the speed of reality, instead transmitted the loss of being near. He grinned, a slow buttering of his lips, turning away from her while the white of his teeth still blinded her wet eyes. She lifted her shirt up, freeing her arms from its sleeves, letting its collar hang on the trunk of her neck. Her mountains of breasts concealed only nominally, she slithered in body rolls that no one looked at. The T-shirt now looked like a garland worn over one entertaining the last shadows of an emptying audience.

Tarisa turned her attention towards another dancer, then another one. Every dancer had their own personality and longing to tell. All moving without speaking, some still seemed more silent than others. *The determinant of their so-called volume is in the empathy that I can give them.* They appeared louder and more prominent if she could spot herself in their movement. Her focus on the ones who kissed, embraced, and danced in groups was distant, like a spectator's, a human watching a different species in a zoo.

Sitting and watching without intervening lengthened her breaths, pruned to be meditative. She enjoyed being passive—if that's what her looking was called. She grew into a stillness as if she were sitting calmly in a frame, how she had earlier observed the men at the library. She wanted to carry the frame back outside, when the show was done, and imagined being contoured by it on the streets, and then on the hospital couch, and in the cornflower blue bathroom with Mia while giving the girl a soft, gentle shower. This frame would allow her to do everything without intense emotions. *I need just this, not even a halo.* She did not need to be holy. She needed only to calmly cruise.

Maybe all I need to do is look at Mia as if she were a show.

CHAPTER 18

Mia as a human performance. If in every interaction, even the ones that should make her angry, she could feel the distance between herself and 'Mia: the show', she might feel less pain raising the child.

She could wake up each day prepared to avoid conversation. If Mia spoke, she could speak back, minimally. She wouldn't have to initiate conversation.

Mia wouldn't have to know what went on in her silence, the way that Chris didn't seem to know all of what went on inside her head. If she kept on being silent for longer and longer, Mia might just come to believe that it was normal.

Chris didn't know, for instance, that her next big question to him was going to be if she could sleep with other men. 'No emotional strings attached,' she thought of explaining, though she could only hope that that would be the case.

Maybe I do want to walk away.

She considered being someone very different when they woke up the following morning—being more passive, hovering over her own life in a state of constant observation. She could maintain her audience status from tonight and bring it into the hospital room, then home, then into the rest of the lives ahead of them. Finally, before they could think about what had happened, she would be old. She would have lived most of her life distant and numb. Numbness was at least not negativity.

Walking back towards the hospital, she considered taking a detour, going anywhere her feet would take her. This was the alone time that she had wanted. The options of things to do were plenty.

I could eat. Eat tofu. Eat tofu at a restaurant. Eat tofu at a restaurant in a mall. For instance.

But her feet guided her directly towards the hospital. The reverse of being in honey, they moved as if swept by a strong current. It might have been that she was not used to having time alone outside at night, that she did not really know how to build it, and once she did not want tofu, tofu at a restaurant, tofu at a restaurant in a mall, she could only go back to the thing that she was used to. Anything else would have taken the effort of imagining.

She had given birth on Thursday and returned to the foundation on Monday. In the contract that she had signed, maternity leave did not exist, for she was a freelancing consultant. It was precisely what Kevin, her line manager, was trying to change in trying for her promotion. With all the work that she did, she deserved more money and more rights.

She also returned to work, her stomach not yet returned to flat, because she liked working. From her starting role as a desktop researcher, she had worked her way into something with a practical touch, assisting Kevin in setting up a programme to distribute grants across Southeast Asia. (She had envisioned being a professor whose research impacted practice, and this was the closest to it that she had come.) She flew her mother and her mother-in-law out in turns to take care of Mia the infant, so that she could go to the office and even on business trips around the region. She had let the foundation freeride on her presence at the World Economic Forum for the PR, as she came back and blogged about their meeting on their website, as if she had gone to represent them.

'We can ask for a raise for you,' Kevin had suggested. The foundation was paying her the equivalent of US$2600 a month while dishing out a thousand dollars an hour to pay her former professors—white, male—for consultancy via Skype. If she was valued and not just a hambone in another questionable power structure, then that was not reflected in her salary. She thought about the wage gap she was learning more about. She should feel empowered to ask for a raise.

'Thank you, Kevin,' she replied.

Mr Ooi sat behind his mahogany desk when she and Kevin went in to ask for her raise the following week. Kevin placed a thick portfolio of her research findings and the projects that they had translated that research into—community education centres and reskilling courses in Thailand, Malaysia, Vietnam, Cambodia, and Indonesia—

in front of Mr Ooi. Kevin began to explain that Tarisa had not been given a raise since the first day that she had joined, though her workload had doubled.

And look, I'm here, not having taken maternity leave, she thought now, inching closer and closer to Stamford Hospital, still somewhat feeling that frame around her body, listening to her present self be fused with the self of her past, as if the former still sat in a place that the latter had never left, where she wished she had said more.

'A raise? No.' Mr Ooi, leaning back in his chair, arms and legs crossed, had looked straight at her, as if he did not see or hear Kevin.

She was surprised at how quick his decision was, and how Kevin had become invisible at that instant.

'You leave at five, yes?' Mr Ooi said.

'Yes,' she said. She could guess where this was going. 'But I come in at eight thirty. I'm the first one in the office.'

'Still, you leave at five.'

She took a breath consciously.

'I know you like taking care of your baby, but don't make taking care of your baby a habit,' he said.

She pressed the elevator button to return to the children's ward now, the push of a button countering the image she recollected of Kevin's pull as he retracted her portfolio with shaking hands.

He had known from the start that it was a lost cause or perhaps he himself was also shocked and fumbled. He mistakenly chose to retreat to think up a new strategy. When it had happened, however, what Tarisa saw was that he did not stand up for her. She had written her resignation letter once they left the room and handed it to Kevin in an envelope, with the impersonal efficiency of a mailman who wanted to move on with his life.

She was sick of this memory, which she knew would never leave her. *'I know you like taking care of your baby, but don't make taking care of your baby a habit.'* She didn't want to forget it, but she also wished it didn't exist. The incident was so brief—just three minutes of her life—and yet it stuck to her and became a defining moment. *Why should it come back so often?*

The nurses let her in after she rang the intercom.

Some trips don't take long.

CHAPTER 19

Her back was pressed against the cold, cornflower blue tiles. She pressed her thumb into the wall and felt the cold enter from her fingertips. In a better version of her life, Chris would be in the bathroom too, holding her against the wall. They would be enjoying each other, her entire back crushed and flattened. But in truth, he was wrapped in his little cocoon, already fast asleep.

Alone for long, then longer, her fantasies sometimes maddened with wildness. The words for the act moved towards violent. Seldom did she think about making love. Often, she thought about fucking. She wanted the intensity of being fucked.

She recalled a night when Mia had seen her crying alone on the bed. The little girl had asked the reason for her tears. When she did not know how to answer, Tarisa briefly imagined explaining that 'grown humans are supposed to want to fuck', and that her father wanted none of that. Since Mia's birth, she had felt, as she had said to Chris a year earlier, 'only a labouring body—for a child and then the home, laundry. No rewards, no fucking for me'.

'I'm sorry,' Chris had answered, looking down.

'What about hormonal therapy instead of "sorry"?'

'I've told you already that I don't want to. It can really mess me up. In the long run, it can even destroy me.'

Leaning against the tiles now, she chose a face of a man from a reel in her head, stowing away Chris' concern for self-destruction and moving on with her night in the practical way she knew how.

She surprised herself. *I'm still thinking about him? After all these years?* He had already become a stepfather to some child. *Maybe I would see him at a class reunion. Maybe I should go, just to see him, to fuck him.*

When it was all over, she looked at the hairs on her body that had grown around her pubis and navel. Mia had once followed her into the bathroom during her shower and asked, 'Why do you have hair there?'

'Adults have hair there so that when they make babies, it won't hurt when the Mommy's and Daddy's bodies rub,' she said. Her own use of the present tense unsettled her. She was not someone for whom this applied. Taking this reply for normal, Mia then undressed, too, asking to shower together. She watched water cascading down Tarisa, down the long strands of pubic hair that were clumped together. A few seconds later, she grabbed a toy pail, set it down between Tarisa's feet, and collected the water sliding off her mother's hair. Tarisa let her play, glad that her pubic hair was of some use.

The bush was protruding over her bikini line now. It had been, for months, and she had been conscious to preserve it as a protest against the 'cleanliness' that many men apparently wanted and as an acceptance that her own man didn't want anything. The presence or the absence of unruly hairs made no difference in her partnered life. More than once, she had tried shaving it in case a smooth glow would entice Chris. Always, he looked right through her the way he would a newly polished window.

'Does it matter how I look down there?' she asked after those shaving attempts.

'No. You can be yourself,' he said. When he held her hand at night, letting her fall asleep connected to him, she was both thankful and revolted by the life they had, how it was both beautiful and hopeless all at once.

She now walked to the basin to wash her hands.

Scrubbing a finger that should have been my husband.

CHAPTER 20

The clock said it was half past five in the morning. Chris and Mia were still asleep.

Tarisa considered reading on the cot using her phone's flashlight. She knew it would be uncomfortable, likely very clumsy, to have to hold a phone in one hand and the novel another. She dismissed the idea, recalling that the coffee shop below was open.

Gently, she lowered the cot rails, hoping that the clicking wouldn't bother Chris. She made sure not to slip when her socks touched the ground. A bruised body could mean many days of physical malfunctioning, which would not be helpful to anyone. She looked to see if Mia's thumb was in her mouth, forgetting that the arm board would already have prevented that. When she saw the arm board, she lifted the rails back up until they clicked again, tiptoeing to the bathroom and pulling down one of the bras she had hung inside. It was not lacy, but solid and utilitarian, like all of hers.

She put on an old black maternity shirt that now looked like a tunic, while deciding between sneakers or slippers. It was too dark to put on the sneakers easily, so she chose the slippers. Chris wasn't using them now. It was he who normally used them while she walked around the room in socks.

She grabbed a book that she assumed was the Tanizaki and opened the door, expecting to greet the nurses with a smile, but when she closed the door behind her, their station was empty.

She walked down the quiet hallway, trying to see how many rooms were occupied. Was there a community of troubled parents in here? How many families were in their rooms-cum-cubicles, isolated but living similar lives? If she could spot another parent, she might see herself in them, the way she had seen herself in the dancer with the bob. And if she saw herself in someone else, then she might feel a part of something larger, without having to make a concentrated effort at conversation.

All the rooms in the corridor were unlit. Dark windows made sure the only reflection she saw was her own.

She pressed the button for the ward's double doors to swing open, looking at the garden as soon as she was outside. Leaves took on the weight of dewdrops glistening under a fading night. Calmness and self-expansion powered her to glide through the hallway. She imagined the air behind her gathering into a cape and propelling her forward.

She pressed a button to call the elevator. Lime green lit up its contours. After a silent wait, the doors sliced opened, and she slipped in, resting her head against the wall. Wakefulness and somnolence supplanted each other in intervals. She did not try to control them, letting each live freely. A need to plan for energy did not exist. At home, she would have to plan, but now, Stamford surrounded her. If later, she needed rest, she could be on the cot, curled up next to Mia, pushing buttons that brought in help.

The elevator opened to a quiet lobby on the ground floor. She was glad to see no one, glad to have a space to play inside her head. Using again the sort of questionable calculations that she did the previous day, she saw square grids in her mind, thinking about how one small action of hers had a ratio of mattering relatively big, right here, right now—a blink, for example.

My blinking takes up more room here compared to my blinking in a busy room.

She imagined taking off the cape that she had felt was propelling her forward, now interested in walking as if the honey from Edwina's movement exercise was still stuck to her. The gentle race between wakefulness and somnolence was not over, and in fact, became the cause for flashes of thought that sometimes appeared more dreamlike.

If honey were really around my feet and ankles right now, I'd walk—

A thought she didn't finish when she saw the café. The woman behind the counter was transferring colourful cakes into a large display. *Electric colours.* She was sliding Mia's favourite, rainbow cake, into disciplined grids. Honey left Tarisa's mind. It yearned for a slice of the rainbow for Mia. Then, because the spread was attractive, she eyed the rest: steady, unfaltering white frosting on chocolate shells, dark blueberry sauce halted where it had swum into a batter of cream cheese. She got closer and closer.

Suddenly, a group of men and women in loud prints of designer clothing appeared. Tarisa, who had almost reached the register, put herself in line behind them. They plodded towards a decision of what to order, their slow, democratic discussion oppressing her existence behind.

She gazed down towards the book in her hands, hoping to read it and kill time. That was when she realized the mistake that had been sitting there quietly. In searching for the book in the dark, she had mistakenly picked up Chris' book on jazz harmonization instead of the Tanizaki. Still, she flipped through, in case she could convince herself to have an interest, but words that seemed at ease in their house of pages, such as 'chords', 'dominants', and 'interpolations', made her shut the book as she would the door of a mistaken apartment.

'Takeaway, please,' she said of the rainbow cake when it was her turn, the people from the previous group already settling into their seats, bringing their phones out and no longer speaking to one another.

The need to order a coffee for herself had disappeared, now that the right book was not in reach. She could not be awake for the Tanizaki now. The nurses could already be in the room, doggedly trying to measure Mia's vital signs. If Mia became difficult, she would disrupt Chris' sleep.

By now, it was clear to Tarisa that she was not meant to be awake, that this dawn, things would not go according to her plans. Her senses, while walking back towards the ward, felt dull. Ears that were meant to hear, eyes that were meant to see, skin that was meant to feel, felt shrunken, closed off, and she realized that the brief journey to the café was not the start of her day, but an eventful interval in the middle of her night, where she had followed one impulse after another, to wind up with a rainbow cake for Mia—delightful, but unplanned.

CHAPTER 21

The sun was out now, pigmenting the room's curtains bronze. She remembered feeling lucky that she had caught the nurses in time, just as they were about to enter the room.

'How was it, last night?' Chris asked from the sofa, his blanket folded by his side. Using a sliver of sunlight, he was reading the *The New Yorker*.

Good, he's got energy, focus. He slept well.

His voice sounded clear, coming from a body that had already warmed up for the day. He must have been up for some time already.

But the curtains are still closed. To let me sleep.

'Thanks for keeping the curtains closed. You could have opened them,' she said.

'No problem.'

'The show was good, it was great.' She closed her eyes and pressed her fingers on her eyelids.

'Glad to hear that.'

Her head on the pillow, she scanned what she could of her surroundings. She couldn't see any breakfast, though she smelled butter. 'Did you sleep well? What time is it?'

'Not too bad. Quarter to eight.'

She shook her head and widened her eyes. She rolled her eyes clockwise to wake them up, like the movement of a clock she was seeing in her head. The hand moved round and round in countless circles, wiping away time. This morning or afternoon, she would need to find an hour to proofread her friend's writing as a favour. Apart from that, time would not be a part of her concerns.

'Feel free to go get sunlight or something, Chris,' she yawned.

He came up to kiss her. 'I love you.'

'I love you too.' She waited a little for her words to sink in, so that they wouldn't seem perfunctory. Lately, she sometimes felt they were. And because true love did not speak curtly, she added, 'I actually went down once already to get something. If you need coffee or whatever, feel free to go get some. Don't feel like you need to stay. Mia's asleep anyway.'

He seemed to realize something immediately after she said that. She wondered what it was but didn't want to seem too eager and ask. 'I'll go now,' he said. Tarisa watched him put on a new pair of pants. As he wriggled into them, she saw the little soft knob of a penis in his boxers and looked away. 'Do you want anything?'

'No, no thank you. Maybe I'll have a sip of whatever you're having when you're back.' She smiled at him.

'I love you,' he said again, opening the door.

She turned away as he left the room. She slid off the cot, put the rail back up until it snapped and pressed it down to make sure that Mia would be safe inside. She went to the bathroom and sat on the toilet seat, staring at the walls. She pretended to blow bubbles, imagining herself in a pool.

She heard the door open and wheels and machinery rolling into the room. She didn't know why the nurses were here again. She quickly wiped herself and pulled up her pants, feeling a moist patch sinking into her underwear. She had done a bad job of wiping, the kind she would tell Mia to improve on. She rushed to open the bathroom door to announce that she was present, using the web between her thumb and index finger to push the door handle down.

'Good morning,' she said when she saw Geetha, who looked wordlessly at her.

'Morning, ma'am,' Geetha said after a moment of silence. 'We just need to check her temperature and blood pressure.'

The 'her' in there is Mia. Mia has a name.

Geetha walked towards Mia and lowered the rails halfway. Tarisa guessed that they wouldn't be here for long. After clipping a monitor on Mia's finger, Geetha patted her bottom. Mia started to wake up and tried to move her right hand to her face to suck her thumb, but the arm board hit her chin. She lowered her arm to her side, furrowing her brows though she otherwise looked barely conscious.

'Sweetie, it's okay. It's just blood pressure and temperature,' Tarisa said, standing by the cot, her hands dangling by her side, careful to not touch Mia since she still hadn't washed her hands.

Geetha dug a thermometer into Mia's ear and pressed a button. 'Thirty-seven point five. Much better, ma'am. It looks like the medicine is working.'

'That's good,' Tarisa said.

Geetha tucked the thermometer back into her pocket. Tarisa read the hands of her watch as the back of her wrist turned towards her. It was five minutes to eight.

'After breakfast, ma'am, we'll give her medicine. Please notify us when she's eaten. Before eight thirty would be good, ma'am. They're coming now with the breakfast.' Geetha raised the rail again.

'Sure, no problem,' Tarisa said, although the time frame felt a little ambitious to her.

Once Geetha left, Tarisa elbowed open the bathroom door and went back inside to wash her hands. She turned the water on high, so that the rushing sound would help to wake Mia up.

When she came out, Mia's eyes were open. 'Do we go home yet, Mommy?'

'Good morning, Little Mia. We're not going home yet, sweetie, but you're getting better, which means we'll get to go home soon. Maybe tomorrow,' she said. She caressed Mia's cheeks. She suddenly remembered, watching her index finger curl slowly onto Mia's soft skin, as if in slow-motion, the Vahlen show and therefore the idea that this gentleness was not supposed to exist. Just the previous night, she had wanted it all gone and to view Mia as a performance, but now that desire to be just an observer was not acting. Her caress was leaking warmth and active love, as if she had abandoned her new mission.

Shit.

'But I want to go home now,' Mia said.

'I know. I know you do, but the doctor still needs to see how you feel.'

Should I be speaking more curtly, not caring so much?

And why did I buy her that rainbow cake if I was wishing I should care less?

I had forgotten.

An exhausted mother relapsing into tenderness did not appear logical. Tarisa looked outside the window at the moving clouds.

Clouds also are not logical. But they have some kind of function. At least your mistake is not that you are yelling. You are mistakenly, actively loving.

'Why are you looking at the clouds so long, Mommy?'

What am I supposed to say? 'Have you ever wondered if a cloud would ever fall from the sky and crush you, Mia?' *That didn't sound like the right thing.*

'No.'

Just continue to talk. She's fine with it.

'I'm surprised humans aren't scared of clouds. If I had never seen one and saw one, I'd be afraid of this massive thing that looked like it could fall and crush me.'

'I'm not scared of clouds.'

Change the topic. 'What do you like more—morning or night?'

'Why?'

'I'm just wondering if you have a preference, and if so, why.'

'Morning.'

'Why?'

'I can play.'

Tarisa grunted playfully, thinking of Barbies.

'Do you like morning, Mommy?'

Tarisa wondered, too, looking for answers in the frothy cumulonimbus clouds.

'I think I like night,' she said when something about their lift and flow made them too detachedly wise. Night skies felt humbler, even a little lost, especially when light pollution eclipsed the stars.

She was appreciating this conversation, her and Mia getting to know each other, daughter and mother, like this. Tarisa liked that she didn't have to be someone else, she didn't have to be Barbie, for Mia to be interested in who she was.

There was a sweet spot where conversations would end, and just now it had ended there.

CHAPTER 22

From the earlier smell of butter, Tarisa could guess who and what was coming through the door. The familiar dining services staff entered with a smile and a bow, her face still made up like a Barbie's. On the tray, fried white rice rose with cubes of peach-pink sausage. *Barely any vegetables.*

The woman placed the tray down and prolonged her smile.

A short moment later, Chris angled in, his head and shoulder first, as if he were spying. He held a disposable cup. A Starbucks bag hung on his wrist. Tarisa was surprised to see it. He normally didn't go there and preferred brandless *kopi*, which was cheaper and still delicious.

She didn't know what could be inside the bag. She thought not to ask while the other woman was still here. She also wondered if she should even ask now that she was trying to live merely as an audience of her own life. Although that passivity was meant to apply to situations with Mia, she thought Chris could be someone for practice.

He playfully raised his eyebrows at her. She guessed that he had brought her a quiche or a cake.

'Would you like coffee, tea, juice?' the dining services woman asked, not understanding the silent conversation between the man and his wife.

'Coffee please,' Tarisa said.

'Sir?'

'It's okay, nothing for me.'

'Black,' Tarisa said, pre-empting questions about milk or sugar.

'Crackers? Cookies?'

'Crackers, please.'

'No, Mom, I want cookies!' Mia interrupted.

But they're not for you.

'Mom, I'd like cookies, *please*,' Tarisa cued her.

'Mom, I want cookies, *please*,' Mia said.

'Can we change that to cookies, please?' Tarisa said. 'And can you,' she turned back to Mia, 'please be polite and say good morning to Auntie, Mia?' There was still a role to play, the role of the mother teaching her child manners.

This part cannot be more passive. It would lead to a rude, spoiled grown-up.

'Good MORNING!' Mia shouted and made a silly face.

'Good morning, girl-girl,' the woman replied. She smiled sweetly, then turned back towards her supplies. 'Cookies, of course, ma'am.'

'Thank you.'

'Enjoy your coffee, ma'am.' She rested the coffee down onto the desk. 'Where are you from, ma'am?'

Tarisa's gut feeling was right. The woman wanted to linger. The woman was curious.

'Bangkok,' she said hesitatingly.

'But you speak very good English.'

Tarisa knew that she hadn't code-switched, sounding thoroughly American. It had been a quickly calculated decision—the woman was not a taxi driver whose curiosity she would be stuck with for long; the woman was not her condo manager who might have resented gentrifying foreigners from the West.

'I lived in America for many years,' Tarisa explained.

'Very cute girl, ma'am,' she changed the subject, smiling at Mia.

'Thank you. Do you have a daughter too?' Tarisa asked, to make polite conversation. She didn't want her to think they were stuck-up. It felt unkind and unnecessary to create distance because one person was presumably much richer, and therefore worthy of some sort of distance. But what Tarisa was also thinking was that if the other woman was a mother and appeared sane, *that's more proof that mothering doesn't need to make me crazy.*

'Yes, ma'am, but she is already big. She's twenty, ma'am.'

The woman must have been no more than forty herself.

'That's big.'

'Yes, ma'am. Very big. She has her own life already.'

'Mommy, I want the cookies,' Mia interrupted.

'Yes, Mia, soon.'

'Okay, girl-girl. Enjoy your breakfast, ma'am.'

Tarisa looked for her name on the name tag. 'Thank you, Hnin Hnin. Mia, can you say, "Thank you, Auntie Hnin Hnin"?'

'Tagoo!' Mia said and laughed.

'Properly, Mia.'

'Tagoo!' Mia said again.

'Mia.' Tarisa was firm.

'Thank you,' Mia said, disappointed.

'By the way, ma'am? Where in America, ma'am? I also want to go to America.'

'Washington DC, Boston . . .' Tarisa listed.

'Washington . . . Boston . . .' she repeated. 'Is Washington or Boston good, ma'am?'

Is Washington or Boston good? Is Washington or Boston good compared to what?

'They're okay,' Tarisa said. 'I don't know, what do you think, Chris?'

'They're good. Good food, nice cities,' he said to the woman.

'My daughter also want to go to America. Here, we are nothing. There, we go, we may be something. Maybe go find a job, open restaurant. Here, this is all we can be.'

Tarisa nodded slowly. 'Maybe,' she said. 'Maybe.'

When Hnin Hnin disappeared, Tarisa saw how she had practiced a bit of passivity, answering questions minimally at times. It didn't yield a verbal style that she foresaw as eternal. She thought she had answered Hnin Hnin's questions as if she had been a schoolgirl facing multiple-choice questions or an antiquated lady of the manor offering limited choices for the set-up of a tea party.

Neither image felt even remotely close to the one she had of herself.

Mia ate the cookies, leaving crumbs on the cot. Tarisa brushed them off onto the floor and slid into slippers, which Chris was not using. She felt their bumpy soles as she walked purposely on the crumbs. At home, irritated, she would have gathered the crumbs into her palm and thrown them into the bin while giving Mia an earful.

As she slowly crunched them with her feet now, her arms rose. She began to push an imaginary cart of trays towards the clouds that were growing outside. She pictured the long polyester sleeves of Hnin Hnin's uniform feeling boxy around her arms, the cuffs clicking against her wrists, her bony fingers and palms the only part of her limb in contact with fresh air.

In seventeen or eighteen years, when Mia is twenty, maybe I'll be rolling breakfast trays around hospitals myself.

She shared her thought with Mia and Chris.

'Why?' Mia asked, while Chris laughed.

She did not answer Mia, although in talking more to Chris, she also answered Mia's question— 'Not a bad thing, right? We don't need money. I just don't want to be bored.'

'Nah, you'll do something greater,' he said.

'Greater.' That coming from you. 'Really? Actually, I might be fine rolling trays along.' She mimicked the action, faster, more comically for him now. She wasn't sure which Chris she was performing for: the friend, the enemy, or both. The more she thought about her joke, the more sincerely she felt about it. No other path appeared in sight. The upsides to working in Dining Services did

though: colleagues to ward off loneliness, a clear task, and some, nominal pay. She could find job satisfaction the way he had said he did.

'No, really, you'll do something better,' he said again, *meaning so well, remarking so innocently about my future.*

'Like what?' She heard her voice that came out almost as a bark and was surprised by it herself. She tried again, knowing that she should push down the resentment in case he really had a good idea. 'What's possible?'

'I don't know, but you'll find something.'

She lowered her arms and crossed them over her chest. Then, she began to walk, picking up loose objects here and there. Mia had not asked her again, 'Why?' and she felt accepted for that. She liked her more than she liked Chris in this moment.

She took the spoon in her hand and scooped up a pea-sized amount of rice, bringing it to Mia's lips.

'I do my own, Mom.'

'With your left hand? You can?' Tarisa asked.

Mia nodded, and Tarisa turned the spoon in her own hand around to give the handle to Mia. She watched as the child tried to grip it with her less practiced muscles.

Mia brought the spoon to her mouth carefully, dropping some rice onto the tray. 'Finished,' she said after her first bite.

'That's it?'

'I am a person who is not hungry.'

'I think you need more food than that.'

'I am a person who is not hungry.'

'Just a little more, Mia,' Chris chimed in.

'Maybe her appetite's really not working because she's sick,' Tarisa said.

Chris followed Tarisa's lead, giving up. She rolled the overbed table away from the cot. Chris took it from her and rolled it even further away. She sat down on the cot and looked at Mia's silhouette against the sunny window. She had become a blob outlined by the oversized hospital gown. 'All right, sweetheart,' she turned to Mia, wanting to be near her, 'then if you're done with your food, let's do your hair. It's a mess.'

She gripped the base of the ponytail that Chris had tied the previous night.

Mia's hair was thin and silky, unlike her own thick and coarse hair. She pinched a small part of the hair tie. 'Hold still, Mia,' she said when Mia began to lean forward.

'Ouchie!'

'It's because you're leaning forward. Why are you leaning forward? Don't lean forward.'

'Ouchie!'

'Not really, sweetie. Come up now. Stay tall and straight.'

Mia popped back towards her. Tarisa adored her straightened back. How alert it seemed made her want to laugh. She smirked and loosened Mia's hair tie by pulling it straight towards herself.

'Ouchie! Mommy, no! Don't make my hair ouchie!'

'It's not ouchie. I'm being gentle to your skull. The ouchie's in your imagination.'

'Ouchie!' Mia cried even more loudly.

She combed through Mia's hair with her fingers.

'Mia, be grateful. Augustine doesn't have people doing her hair like this,' Chris said, coming to stand by Tarisa's side.

Chris, stop it. It's going well.

'Sweetheart? Do you want to know what a real ouchie would be?'

'No, Mom.'

'I mean not a big one, just one so you would know what a real ouchie would be like.'

'No, Mom.'

'Okay, sweetheart, you know what, I have to do this. I have to do this because if I don't, then you will say "ouchie" every time it isn't ouchie, okay?' Tarisa gave Mia one quick pull by the hair.

'Ouchie!'

'That's what the real ouchie would be like. You see? What I do normally is not an ouchie. You see, if I pull your hair like this,' she tugged a little harder, 'there would be an ouchie. She brushed Mia's hair gently with her fingers. 'But if I just brush it like this, like how I was doing it to you earlier, then?'

'Then no ouchie,' Mia said and laughed.

'See?' Tarisa began to laugh with her.

They repeated it one more time: the tug, the words, the laughter. Chris had not expected it.

You didn't know you didn't need to save me this time. I've got a mother's love. I've been so much happier here; it's less tiring, can't you see?

A brief knock sounded after a ponytail perched high on Mia's head.

Whatever just happened felt energizing, warm, nice.

Doctor Dhivya and Geetha walked in before Tarisa could let them in. The doctor was bursting in tight dark jeans, which indicated a weekend. *Saturday.* Tarisa had briefly lost track of time.

Mia's lips began to tremble. The rest of her body froze. Tarisa pulled her in with both arms. The root of her ponytail itched Tarisa's nose. Tarisa quickly jerked her face away, careful to not loosen her grip.

The doctor's going to ask about medicine. Mia still hasn't really eaten.

'Good morning. It seems like she's responding well to the IV drip,' the doctor said. She came to stand at the foot of the cot. She looked at the clipboard Geetha handed her. Tarisa waited to hear whether the doctor would call Mia by her name, or if it did not seem to matter to her. 'We'll keep her on it,' the doctor continued.

No, she's not using her name. We are nothing but generic patients to her.

'And we'll continue to monitor her temperature, blood pressure, and all the vital signs.'

'Will we need to stay another night?' Tarisa kept her words spaced out and her voice low to hide her eagerness, especially from Chris, who had not said anything except a quiet, 'Good morning, Doctor.'

'We'll see how the lab test comes out today. It's Saturday, so the results might be slow.'

She's equivocating. She thinks I don't want to stay another night.

Tarisa turned to him. Chris nodded slowly. She tried to process his reaction. She watched his Adam's apple moving up and down.

'Okay,' he replied faintly.

Even if they had expected a two-night stay from the beginning, the reality of it still seemed heavy for him. Tarisa quickly tried to calculate what might be suboptimal for him here. *Bed, lack of fresh air, food.* The bed, she could not change. The lack of fresh air was up to him to find. The food, she might be able to work on. She imagined his morose expression as he would be served another hospital lunch and dinner today, and then another breakfast and lunch the following day.

That's many rounds of mediocrity. More pineapples would not make up for that.

Tarisa brought one arm away from Mia and placed a hand on Chris' back for him to feel some comfort. She didn't say a word about herself feeling thrilled or her trying to make sure that this place would be good to him, so that she could continue to stay overtly happily.

'So, what's in the bag?' she asked as soon as they were alone again.

'Cake,' he said.

'Oh, shoot. I forgot I also bought Mia cake,' she said. She turned towards the cake box from the café.

'Cake!' Mia said excitedly, trying to throw her arms in the air, but the arm board stopped her.

'*Now* she's hungry,' Tarisa said teasingly.

'Yum, yum! Cake!' Mia sang.

Tarisa opened the box and flattened out the sides. She put the cake next to Mia's barely touched breakfast. 'Using just your left hand's really fine?'

Mia nodded.

Tarisa looked inside the Starbucks bag to find the cake that Chris had mentioned. 'What?' she asked when she saw what was there.

'Mommy, cake!'

'One sec, Mia. Chris, what's this? I don't understand,' Tarisa said as she stared at the cylinder.

CHAPTER 23

'Cabergoline,' he said.

'What?' Tarisa said, confused.

'It's a surprise for you. I've been coming to see the urologist. Here.'

'What?' Tarisa repeated.

'To correct my hormones.'

'What's that, Mommy?'

'Daddy's medicine for his sick penis, sweetheart,' Tarisa quickly answered. 'For how long, Chris?'

'It's been a few months.'

'How many?'

'Four.'

'Why's his penis sick?'

'It doesn't move like it should, sweetie.' Tarisa turned the bottle around and around. 'So, you went to see the urologist just now?' She was confused. It seemed too early in the day.

'No, actually, I just went down to the pharmacy to pick up the prescription. It's actually a drug the urologist couldn't dispense from his office directly.'

'A special drug. You mean extremely potent?'

'Yeah, apparently.'

'What does it do?'

'It helps get and maintain an erection.'

'How?'

'Not sure, exactly. Something about dopamine receptors.'

Tarisa was trying to understand. He was usually extremely careful about what he put in his body. She also wondered why she hadn't seen the effects on his libido if he had already been coming here for four months.

'Has it been—I mean those doctor's visits—have they been,' she didn't know what word to use, 'working?'

'Um, yes and no. The hormones are where they should be, but I still don't really feel like, you know, *Oh I need to have sex*, so I told the doctor about it, and he said that this should help. This one,' he pointed to the cabergoline, 'I've never tried, actually. It's used to treat other diseases, but a common side effect is hypersexuality.' Chris laughed.

Tarisa wondered if it wasn't out of nervousness.

'I've read some really crazy things online,' he said.

Tarisa walked closer to Mia, holding the cabergoline in her left hand. She cut a small piece of cake with her right and brought it up to Mia's lips. The rainbow colours were boldly artificial, distracting.

'Mommy, I said I eat my own,' Mia reminded her.

'Oh, sorry, I forgot.' She put the spoon down. She turned to Chris and looked at him silently for a second. She imagined him chasing her around the house and treating her like a sex doll. She tried to calm herself down.

'Hypersexuality would be a side effect for people whose libido baseline was at the normal level though, right? So, the idea is that, since you're beginning at a lower baseline, your libido would be raised to a normal level. Is that right?'

'Yummy!' Mia said. Tarisa turned to look at her. Her mouth was full. Her teeth were covered in the colours of a rainbow.

'Right,' Chris confirmed.

'But you don't know exactly how it works?'

'Right.'

'But you would become sexual or hypersexual.'

'Possibly.'

She did not want to become his sex doll.

'Wait, and where's the cake you bought me?' Her brain was firing in many ways. She was trying to maintain both lightness and heaviness. Perhaps she was asking about the cake out of nervousness too.

'Oh, just kidding. There was no cake. Sorry. I just walked into Starbucks to get a bag, pretended to be a customer. Adds to the surprise, doesn't it?'

'It's okay. This is better than cake.' She realized that she meant it. 'What else did you read about it? Ca—what?' She was worried.

'Cabergoline. Some people get into gambling. Irritability,' his voice trailed off, indicating that he was speaking from a much longer list.

'Gambling?'

'Yeah.'

'We live within walking distance of the casino, Chris. We just drove by it yesterday morning. I don't know if this is a good idea. What else?'

'Can I see?' Mia reached out her arm.

'One sec, sweetheart,' Tarisa looked at the drug label again. 'What else, Chris?'

'Well, some wives have complained about, you know, things like their husbands seem to have become emotionless,' he said. The last word there arrested her. 'They don't seem to love them any more, or they just want to have sex all the time. That kind of stuff. One guy in a forum said his sex drive was so high that he began cheating on his wife.'

Tarisa's eyebrows rose. She imagined Chris in a dingy brothel, an experienced woman on top of him, teaching him techniques.

Not a bad idea. It's what he needs. More techniques.

'You'll be in the red-light district? Or with one of your colleagues?'

'No, no, I mean, it won't happen to me,' he said.

'You never know, Chris. Finasteride's side effects were also not supposed to happen to you.'

'True.'

'Mommy, can I see?' Mia interrupted.

Tarisa handed the bottle to Mia. 'Don't shake, sweetie. In case it breaks,' she said.

'Is it candy?' Mia asked.

'No!' Tarisa and Chris said at the same time, almost as a shout.

'Never eat stuff that comes from bottles like this, okay?' Chris said.

'It's medicine. You can get really sick or die if you eat it,' Tarisa said.

Mia laughed. 'Okay.'

'Wait, so this thing,' Tarisa said to Chris, trying to hold the conversation with him while also hearing the flurry in her own head. She fed Mia another spoonful of cake. 'I don't get it. You're willing to risk all those side effects?'

She thought about how he had rattled off the list, enumerating 'emotionless' and then 'sex drive . . . so high' right after, as if he couldn't see how impactful these effects would be. It was the possible ruin of their marriage that he was presenting.

'Yeah, I mean, for us, you know,' he said.

'I thought you were afraid of Western medicine and stuff like this. Understandably. That stuff messed you up years ago.'

'Yeah, but I thought I could try. Again, you know.'

Why now, after all the refusal of hormone therapy?

She didn't understand what triggered his change. 'Isn't there anything milder? So, this is better than hormone therapy?'

'I think so.'

'Have you asked your doctor?'

'Yeah, sort of.'

'What do you mean?'

'I've done hormone therapy actually.'

'What?'

'Yeah, I've been taking hormones, but they don't seem to work.'

She saw his disappointment, his frustration at himself. He was not a man who would ever harm himself. The fact that he had tried hormone therapy, even knowing that it could change him for the worse, proved he wanted to make the effort.

'I've tried. I've been pumping my penis, taking tadalafil daily, doing pelvic exercises, too,' he said. His voice trailed off again.

'What's pumping your penis?'

'It's when I use this tool, like a vacuum. I put my penis inside and pull it, and it helps to, you know, get an erection. It trains my body to allow the blood in.'

'Oh,' Tarisa said.

I can't imagine it.

'What? What's that, Daddy?' Mia asked.

'A penis pump sweetheart,' Tarisa quickly answered. 'It allows Daddy's *joot-joo*—' she used the Thai word for children now, because it sounded cuter '—to stand up. Men need their *joot-joo* to stand up to make babies and do more things with their wives.'

'Are you having more babies?' Mia asked.

'No, sweetheart, no. This is not about babies. This is the "doing more things with their wives" part.'

'Oh,' Mia said. 'What things?'

'Sleeping together in happy ways, Mia,' Tarisa said.

'Daddy needs a pump?'

'Yes, Daddy needs a pump,' Tarisa said while looking at Chris, trying to imagine a vacuum sucking him in.

'So, what do you think, T? Cabergoline! I think it could be great!' He clapped his hands together and puffed out his chest.

She couldn't help but imagine him irritable—arguing with her, clicking his tongue at her, shouting at her, hitting her—and then running away in the middle of the night to gamble. She didn't want to have to explain to a beast that he used to be sweet and calm.

Tarisa could tell that Chris was ready to move forward, towards a future that he imagined could be better, but Tarisa wasn't sure if she shared his optimism. If everything had failed and all that was left was this pill from the urologist, then . . .

She turned and trimmed off another small piece of the cake, sweeping together the crumbs with the edge of the fork until they all clustered. She spoke, trying to let her voice catch up with his enthusiasm. 'It could be good,' she said, against the fear in her head. She swept up the crumbs and watched them fall between the tines. 'But why are you suddenly okay with this kind of risk?'

'I mean, it's not so suddenly, right? I've been seeing the urologist for a while,' he said.

'Why?' Tarisa asked.

'For you! For us!' he said as if it were obvious.

'Why?' she asked again.

'I also wanna, you know, like, sleep with you.'

'You do?' She couldn't believe it. How had a man who put his nose in a book every night, reading several inches away from his wife, who was sometimes naked, waiting on the bed, ever hinted at that?

The way he's been sleeping on the sofa here is like the way he sleeps on the queen bed every night.

'Yeah, T! Of course, I do! You're my wife! Mia, can I have it back now, please?' he asked, stretching his hand out to her. 'Yeah, so, what do you think?' he turned back to Tarisa.

'I think—' she didn't want to disappoint him '—I think it could be good,' she said.

In the bathroom, after she showered, Tarisa tied her wet hair into a high bun. She felt the annoying cloy of water at the top of her nape. There was no hair dryer in the room—a reminder that the hospital wasn't, after all, a hotel. She inhaled and held her breath, trying to imagine having no more access to air.

If I were dead, I wouldn't have to think about this cabergoline.

She heard noise from outside. The nurses had come back in again to give Mia her medicine. Mia was crying and screaming, but Tarisa thought it best to stay in the bathroom until it was all done. She shouldn't have to worry about Mia. Chris was outside with her.

After she heard them leave, she came out with the towel around her neck to keep the hair from wetting her T-shirt. She was surprised to see Chris on the couch, not as near Mia as she had expected him to be. Tarisa sat next to him, angling for a patch of sunlight that could dry her hair.

'Mommy! Mommy!' Mia cried. Tarisa shot back up to hug her and pat her back.

Mia's nose was red from crying.

'What are you up to now?' Tarisa asked Chris, warming Mia up with her body but knowing that Mia would calm down faster the less she made a big deal of what had just happened.

'Probably *The New Yorker.*'

'Again?' Tarisa said.

'Yeah.'

'You've been so good about your medicine. Would you like some cartoons?' Tarisa asked Mia.

Mia nodded. Tarisa looked at the redness at the tip of her nose again. She pulled Mia in for another hug.

With one hand around Mia, she used the other hand to turn on the television. 'I'm gonna be sitting on the couch with Daddy, doing something for my friend, okay?'

'What thing?' Mia asked.

'Proofreading.'

'What's that?'

'Correcting little errors that people make.'

'Why?'

'Because Laura, my friend, asked me to,' Tarisa said, then turned up the television volume.

Mia nodded wordlessly, already mesmerized by the screen, which was showing *Sophia the First.*

Tarisa put her laptop on her knees and entered her long-time password, Iloveresearch123! She often thought about changing it, but for convenience, the familiar password prevailed.

'I need to do that thing for Laura,' Tarisa tried to tell Chris, even though he was already absorbed in his reading.

She reread her friend's message to make sure she knew what she was supposed to do. 'Hey, Tarisa! I know you're super busy with Mia, but if you wouldn't mind, can you please, please help me look over my work? I know you don't write fiction, but since you're a really good writer in general, can you please help me look over this short story? I don't want to give it to another writer. The competition is fierce! XOXO, Laura. P.S. DC misses you.'

Yeah, Laura, don't write emails that show me you don't proofread.

She got up and moved the tray of food off the overbed table to the floor, a little anxious about the amount of work she'd be having. *To do for free.* She wiped the table surface once with a tissue, put her laptop on top, and rolled it over closer to the sofa. 'Would you like to lay down and put your legs up?' She sat down and asked Chris. She knew he liked to read lying on his back, with his feet on the couch. He would never bring his legs up onto her thighs without her saying that it was fine, and he accepted her invitation now. His legs were heavy, but she liked their heat.

In Laura's document, Tarisa changed tenses from past to present, added the necessary hyphens and punctuations for pauses. So far, it was not as bad as she had thought. If Tarisa passed through paragraphs without making any changes, she would reread them to make sure that she hadn't missed anything. Even after Laura's manuscript had convinced her that her friend was indeed capable of some proofreading, Tarisa's conscientiousness would not let any perfection go unquestioned.

'Mommy, can you make it louder?' Mia asked, looking at the television.

'Mia, Mommy needs to concentrate,' Chris said before Tarisa could answer.

'It's fine, Chris. Just commas and periods.' Tarisa kept her eyes on her computer. 'But thanks,' she added, hoping it didn't sound too much like an afterthought.

'Mom!' Mia was impatient.

'Mia, Mom's working,' Chris said.

'Chris, could you please?' Tarisa asked.

Chris reached out to the remote control and increased the volume to the next bar.

'I can't hear it!' Mia shouted.

'Already increased it,' Chris said, readjusting his hands on his magazine. Tarisa used Mia's interruption to break her own concentration on Laura's document. She succumbed to an impulse she had been trying to suppress. 'C,' her index finger pecked the keyboard. Her pinkie slowly followed, 'a'. Then, faster and faster, other letters hurried in, speeding to make a word before a part of her could interrupt.

Chris got up to use the bathroom and she followed. She didn't need it, but it had just seemed like a good excuse to hang out while Mia's attention was affixed to the television. 'All this fucking pubic hair,' she groaned as she wiped.

'It's fine,' he said.

'It makes it so fucking hard to wipe.'

'It's fine.'

'Maybe I should shave it off. At least trim it.' Thinking about what she had just read on cabergoline, she played with it, combing through with her fingers, watching the hairs stand up as if erected.

Patting them down again, she left the toilet bowl, washed her hands, and watched him aim and pee. She felt ridiculous catching herself feeling envious of his stream.

She didn't know exactly how, but it just seemed to catch his penis' attention in a way no part of her could.

'It's already over, Mia,' Tarisa said, watching the closing credits roll up silently after the last scene, that of Princess Sophia dining with her friends amid a cornucopia.

'No, it's not!' Mia protested.

'Yes, it is. These are called "closing credits". It means the show has ended. It just says who the animators are. Are you interested in who the animators are? Come now, we're done with screen time.' Tarisa pressed the power button.

'I want to eat sausage,' Mia said suddenly, hungered by the cartoon's ending.

'I want to eat sausage too,' Tarisa said, certain she was the only one who heard the double entendre.

'That's weird. You never really eat sausage,' Chris noticed.

'No, I don't,' she said, making sure she didn't look at him, so that he wouldn't see what was on her mind.

Cabergoline would give me sausage.

'How are you doing?' he said, putting his hand on the small of her back.

Tarisa considered possible replies. 'Good,' she said and tried on a smile. 'You?'

CHAPTER 24

After a moment's silence, she could no longer hold it in. 'I don't think it's a good idea.'

'Sorry, what? Were you talking to me?' Chris' face peered from behind his magazine, over the pastel cover portraying busy lives in New York.

'Yeah. I think that cabergoline might not be a good idea.'

'Oh. Why?' He tried to sit up.

She helped him to remove his feet from her thighs so that they wouldn't hit the table.

'It doesn't sound like anything good would come out of it besides sex, like just having sex,' she said.

No forum or website indicated specifically that it would even be good sex.

She silently chided herself for being picky and for considering that good sex might be worth an emotionless husband. 'And you could get, like, a bunch of other side effects.' She turned her screen to him, knowing that these were pages he had likely already read.

'Right,' he said, as soon as he saw what she was looking at. His face took on a serious expression, his eyebrows pressed down by a heavy weight. 'I mean . . .'

She waited for him to finish the sentence, while listening to the reruns of doubts in her mind.

'I mean, yeah, what should we do? I'll do whatever you want me to do,' he said. His words made her wonder if their sex might not always be just hers.

'Let's do no risk,' she said.

'No risk, no reward?' He seemed a little surprised.

'Yeah. No risk, no reward. It's okay. We focus on the no-risk part,' she said, looking at him curling his lips inward, biting down his disappointment.

Those words—'I'll do whatever you want me to do'— were so precious, a partner's commitment to be coveted in and of itself. She could not lose this to a pill. There would be no pill to reverse it.

She recalled the Uzbek man and the woman he was strangling in the parking lot, the men in the documentaries that she saw about domestic violence, her married friends whose husbands were seldom present.

These people had sex regularly, but they did not have a love like Chris'.

He looked at her, waiting for an answer as if he didn't think she could be confused or need time to think through things. She did not know how to handle his dependence on her now. It was bizarre that he let her answer this question when she was the one who felt more dependent on him to have even a basic life.

'Don't,' she said, without looking at him. She wanted to be firm. 'I think don't take it.'

'Okay, then I won't,' he said softly. He seemed taken aback and disappointed.

Did he want to try it?

'How much was it?'

'It's okay. It's not about the money.'

'No, I know. I'm just curious.'

'Forty dollars a pill.'

'Hmm.'

'Even if it were a million, if you don't think it's a good idea, I won't,' he said.

She imagined him having signed a check for a million dollars, trying to see if it would change her mind.

'I'm just imagining our marriage falling apart. Me losing you the way you are,' she said. An impulse struck her. She touched his hand and asked, 'Can you try to hit me?'

'What?'

'I mean, no, don't hit me. Just put your hand up in the air, as if you're going to hit me.'

'No, T, that's crazy!'

'I just want to see what it would feel like. Quick. Mia's not looking.' They looked at Mia, flipping through *The New Yorker*, pausing at a cartoon of two cavemen out on a walk, one asking, 'Did we remember to put out the fire?'

'Come on!'

He grimaced. She knew that he wouldn't do it, so she took his hand and drew it up in the air. His wrist and fingers went limp. She felt his arms grow heavy. She moved his hand close to her cheek and shook his wrist. His limps fingers bounced back before they could strike her skin. He was like a cadaver that she was trying to shape. In the end, only his fingertips grazed her.

'Stiff!' she commanded and uncoiled his fingers. She gripped his palm and put it to her cheek. She tried to knock it hard against her, but he resisted each time it got close.

'Irritable. Gambling. Angry,' she said. She realized that 'angry' was not on the list. She was beginning to make things up. 'No, "angry" is not on the list,' she corrected herself, 'but whatever it is, it's not you.'

She put her laptop on the table, which she rolled away, careful not to put it close to Mia who might knock it off. She stood up and went to stand next to where he sat. His head was an inch away from her chest. The back of her fingers slowly glided onto his temple, his jawline, his chin. His face did not feel soft and round like Mia's. It was more angular and rougher. Her knuckles caressed it. Her other hand touched the back of his head, a huge curve she rarely felt because it was not in their culture that a person should touch the head of someone older.

Her hand covered the empty band where his hair follicles had been extracted to be implanted closer to his forehead. She pulled him in and caressed his crown lightly, grazing through the hard stubs near his forehead. She knew that behind her, Mia was distracted enough, tracing contours of skylines curled with caves, that she wouldn't care to ask what they were doing.

'I love you,' Tarisa said, thinking back to all the ways he had been a husband by being a father.

He hugged her tightly, wrapping the smallness that she physically was.

His cheek softened into her upper belly. 'I love you, too,' he said.

She turned her cheek to rest it on his head. She could feel the oils of his scalp stick to her skin. She didn't understand why he loved her, given all the ways that she was harsh and raw.

She began to rub his back gently, the tempo of her strokes matching a tear that crept down her cheek. She decided to not let him see it, to have the tear just for herself. Yet she saw his eyes on her wet cheek when she unlatched from him a minute later. He didn't ask about it. For a second, she was irritated by his silence. She let the tear continue to trickle. She was sure that he saw it.

What would you want him to ask anyway? You have nothing new to say.

A knock on the door broke their bodies apart.

Once the doctor had chosen her spot, looming right over the foot of Mia's cot, she conveyed the lab results that had come back unusually quickly. The results couldn't pin down anything, but there seemed no cause for concern, especially since Mia was fever-free now and had no new symptoms. They could go home.

Chris nodded to the doctor with a small smile, which confirmed to Tarisa how much he had been wanting to leave. She could hear him thinking about fresh air and good food. She imagined him wanting to say to her—he, who must have known all along that she was enjoying this—'You can't simulate life in here forever. Outside, the way we usually do it, is the way it really is.' He adjusted the curtains after the doctor left, pushing them even further away from each other, until they touched the window frames and rebounded. The increase in brightness was marginal but they did see more people, on corners of streets, which the curtains had earlier blinded them from seeing.

CHAPTER 25

'Sashimi for lunch? We could order in. Celebrate,' Tarisa said. It was half past eleven. Outside, teenage girls held hands with boys they were falling in love with. Parents yanked toddlers across the street. 'It will be a while until we get the discharge procedures done, right?' She remembered that it took almost three hours for the hospital and the insurance company to communicate. Only then would they be able to leave without paying a dime. It was the insurance company that would be footing the bill of thousands of dollars.

'Sashimi's a good idea,' Chris said right away.

They looked on their phones for the menu. Tarisa hadn't seen Chris touch his phone since reading his boss' email the previous day. She admired his ability to be present wherever he went.

Chris enthusiastically read out the names of the dishes that he wanted to eat.

'Should we get anything for Mia?' he asked.

'It might be a waste of money. She's fine with the hospital food anyway.' But on second thought, Tarisa changed her mind. 'Actually, let's get her something more nutritious. That hospital stuff is gross. I mean, I've pre-ordered it, but.'

'No, Mom, I want the sausage,' Mia said.

'Why did I make her ears?' Tarisa muttered, chuckling a little.

'What, Mommy?'

'No, nothing.'

'What, Mommy?'

'Nothing, sweetheart. I said you had good ears.'

'Mom, I want the sausage.'

'The sausage isn't good for you, sweetie. You already had it for breakfast.'

'Yeah, Mia, you already had it for breakfast,' Chris tried to help.

'In fact, you didn't even really eat it, remember?'

'But now I'll eat it,' Mia said.

'Can't you eat something more nutritious?' Tarisa asked.

'No, I like sausage.'

'Chris,' Tarisa said, wanting his help.

'Sausage isn't healthy, Mia. You can't have it every meal. Fish is better for you,' he tried.

'You actually *like* fish, Mia. The grilled *saba* from this place, especially.'

'But I want sausage.'

'Your fondness for them equal,' Tarisa began in a mock-lecturing tone, 'why not pick the healthier one?'

'Fish, Mia, you should have fish,' Chris said.

'No, if you get me fish, I won't eat. I am a person who is not hungry,' Mia said, raising her palms to their faces. She insisted one more time, 'I am a person who is not hungry.'

'I'm getting it,' Tarisa silently mouthed to Chris.

'Something is happening! Mom, something is happening in the phone!' Mia shouted, looking at the phone Tarisa had left by the cot.

An unknown number flashed on the screen. Tarisa answered, following the voice's directions for her to go down to get the food; it wasn't possible for deliverymen to progress beyond the lobby, the voice on the line explained.

She found a man still in a biker's helmet waiting near the ground-floor elevators. He handed her a plastic bag filled with disposable boxes and scuttled across to his motorcycle parked illegally in front of the hospital's main doors.

She remembered reading articles about how deliverymen had to work quickly and worked until they couldn't feel their feet the next day. She imagined being in his shoes, trying to make a living without Chris around, the way she had imagined being like Hnin Hnin. Her identification with these people, who must have dreamt of doing something else, as Hnin Hnin had said she did, could not be stopped.

'No time to waste. It's sashimi. It rots,' she said, not sharing what she had just imagined.

'Yeah, let's eat,' Chris agreed.

'I already eated if you got me *saba*,' Mia said.

'You had a bite of fried rice and rainbow cake. You really need to eat some real food, Mia,' Tarisa said, breaking apart wooden chopsticks.

'Mia, when you're sick, you need food. Your body needs the food to fix what's wrong,' Chris echoed, ripping her mackerel apart with the plastic spoon and chopsticks as best as he could.

This is it. This is what I have, for now.

The sight and smell of grilled mackerel changed Mia's mind. She began to look at the bowl. 'No veggies!' she yelled and waved her hands.

'You need to have veggies, Mia,' Tarisa said and smiled.

'Okay, but small pieces.'

Chris halved each leaf of lettuce for Mia, until the littlest leaves stuck to the tip of his nails. Using the skin between the base of his thumb and index finger, he picked up the fork and pushed the vegetables onto the sticky rice and mackerel skin, making the lettuce unavoidable for Mia's fork.

'Okay, ready,' he said, rolling the overbed table towards her. She looked at the food, and her little nose responded with twitches. The fish smelled of the sea, which she had always liked.

'*Itadakimasu*,' Tarisa said, and Chris followed.

They all plunged in with their fork or chopsticks, smelling the ocean around them.

'Remember our trip to Okinawa?' Mia asked, referring to a trip they had made just a few months ago.

'Yeah. Great trip, right, Mia?' Tarisa asked.

'I love Okinawa. Can we go again? And can we go camping?' Mia asked.

'I'd love to, Mia, but your dad doesn't like camping.'

'We can go without him,' Mia proposed.

'Just you and me, you mean?' Tarisa asked, surprised.

'Yes.'

'You'd be okay going with just me?' Tarisa steadied her gaze on Mia. She wanted to see how real her feelings were. She remembered something that Leela had said: 'Three-year-olds don't lie.'

Mia smiled brightly. Her eyes widened, and she nodded. 'Yes,' she said.

Tarisa grinned. 'That's great,' she said.

'And what would I do if you suddenly die?' Mia suddenly asked.

'If I *die*?' Tarisa asked, a little bewildered. 'Do you know what it really means, to die?'

'No,' Mia answered, pinching a fragment of lettuce out of her mouth. 'But I can see you at home after that.'

They said nothing much as they ate the rest of the meal. The shared appreciation of the food hung in the quietness between bites. Nods passed around their triangle.

Tarisa and Chris sat covering the food from sunlight in case it would spoil the raw fish. They were being overprotective, they realized, but they couldn't help themselves.

'Eating something that has gone bad would mean more time in the hospital,' Tarisa joked, trying to see how Chris would take it.

He shook his head. He swallowed the bite and said, 'Yeah, I can't imagine that.'

He didn't seem to notice that Mia had spilled fish and rice on her bed. Tarisa saw but didn't jump up to clean it as she knew that housekeeping would come. Tarisa imagined the moment when they would open the apartment door and slide into its long entryway. The large lion painting would be waiting at the end of the hallway, and they would be marching like a family of ants towards it. They would then suddenly disperse. Mia would head for her toys; Tarisa would turn towards the bathroom, where she would grab the hamper and drag it to the kitchen to do a load of laundry. Chris might play the piano. Afterwards, he would read to Mia on the couch while he gave her milk from a bottle. Tarisa would continue to do some chores, likely more laundry. Lights if she had done darks or vice versa.

Tarisa assessed her energy. She inhaled and thought about how ready she was to be in the present. And, unlike when she had entered this hospital, she now felt that she could walk through the ward doors and stay out in 'the real world' for another year. She wasn't excited to return to her apartment, but she had reaffirmed for herself in the past two days that this hospital would exist for her if she needed rest in the future. And in between now and her next trip, she had a girl who thought she was good enough to go camping with, just the two of them. This didn't foreshadow less tiring parenting, but it suggested that, so far, her efforts had paid off. Mia liked her.

CHAPTER 26

The wristbands were cut off from their wrists. The needles and arm boards were removed. They said goodbye to the nurses and walked out the way they had come in. They passed the pharmacy.

'Is this where you got the cabergoline?' Tarisa asked Chris.

'Yeah,' he said, still looking a little disappointed.

'It's okay,' she said. 'Even if it had cost you a million dollars, I'd still think I wouldn't want to risk losing you.'

'You really think it will be that bad?'

'I don't know, but it has the potential to be that bad, doesn't it?'

'Yeah, I guess so.'

'What, Mommy, Daddy?' Mia interrupted.

'Daddy found a medicine, but I don't think he should take it,' Tarisa said.

'Why, Mommy?'

'Because it could make him very mean.'

'How mean?'

'Like he-won't-love-us mean.'

'Wow! Mean!'

Tarisa put her hand at the small of Chris' back as they waited for the taxi. He brought his arm around her shoulder and pulled her in. 'I love you,' he said.

'I love you, too.' She meant it.

The taxi came. They drove past the casino. She imagined Chris inside, throwing chips, dice, and cards, or pulling the handles of slot machines.

At home, the lion painting looked the same. The mane was golden like the sun. Tarisa opened the curtains, letting sunlight in. Soon, the sun was covered by clouds. The strait looked rougher, like water almost at a boil. Small boats and large ships responded to a siren that signalled a looming thunderstorm. Tarisa could not see it coming with her naked eye.

She felt ambivalent about an email that she had glanced at in the taxi, which was asking her to forward the message to her 'networks'.

'Grant funding is available to support low-income female artisans in Southeast Asia. Maybe you would know somebody who would like to apply. Please forward,' the message said.

She stood, one leg on the balcony, the other inside, and posted the attached PDF on her Facebook page. She tagged a few friends whom she knew were working at foundations. She had a feeling that without tags, her post wouldn't show up anywhere. The algorithm had probably already determined that she wasn't very relevant any more.

Chris began to read to Mia on the couch. Tarisa began to consider doing laundry.

CHAPTER 27

That night, his thick blanket came up to his face. She didn't think that the bedroom was very cold, but she knew that to him, it was. He had explained once or twice that the paucity of hair made him feel cold easily. She used to think he was exaggerating, until she saw more and more how much he really did want to sleep and had no interest in sex, a thing that could be real only if a body was truly different.

She looked at his lips and his cheeks, which had changed visibly from when they had first met. There were signs of age. The skin looked rougher and dryer. The pores were larger. In a few years, he would be forty—and still working the same job, maybe in the same position. He would, nevertheless, be content. He would have time for his family, reading, and jazz. She, who wanted to go somewhere new with her life, couldn't see where that would be.

If things didn't change, he would be by her side like this every night.

What she wanted was a marriage that would last with a man whom she was attracted to. Did she have it?

She moved closer to his face. She wanted to touch it, but she hesitated because she didn't want to wake him up. She held a finger a hair's breadth away from his nostrils to see how he was breathing. She cherished the air that she felt—warm and long strips. She kept the same distance as her finger moved, gently contouring his jawline.

She took a few seconds to look at him. Then, she turned away, facing the ceiling, watching the thin shadows climbing. There were faint clanging sounds coming from the port. She tried to close her eyes, hoping for her own sleep. She pressed her blanket closer to her body. Because being skin-to-skin would help her to relax, she looked for his hand under his blanket. She touched it gently— one finger first, and then, when she sensed that her touch didn't wake him up, she tried one more. Suddenly, his fingers mounted over her hand. She worried that she had disturbed his sleep. She was afraid that he was trying to stop her from touching him, but then he slipped all five fingers between hers and gently squeezed, such that at every point where their skin came into contact, there seemed to be a message and desire for connection.

He was not angry that she had disturbed his sleep. He could have been, and he was not, and she could not tell if he had chosen to respond the way that he did, or if it came to him naturally. Whichever it was, he loved her. She was to use this love to lull herself to sleep, the way some people fell asleep after climaxing. The way two bodies intertwined and folded into each other after sex, this was supposed to be the oxytocin that put her out.

She closed her eyes and told herself to breathe. There was nothing to do but breathe because breathing, contrary to what the act itself was—letting something in then out—was also an act of sealing off, of closure. She tried to feel nothing but her bare existence, imagining the air go through her nose and into her lungs, then U-turning out. This was it: existence, a hollow, hollow thing, made from wind that cruised through cavities. Every want that emanated out of this was complex, colourful, multilayered, and disastrous, compared to the simplicity of breathing. She acknowledged the life that she wanted and sensed how far away it was from being only breath.

It took her a long time to fall asleep. She did not know more precisely how long, and it didn't matter because time was not a necessary function for a life with nowhere to go. She sat waiting in time's room, realizing now, that that was a life.

When she woke up the next morning, he was on the other side of the bed, covered in his own blanket. As she opened the door, Mia said with a bright smile, 'Mommy!'

'Good morning, Little Mia,' she said, turning to the girl on the mattress on the floor.

Epilogue

She showed up at the café of Regina's choice in a linen dress. She arrived first, on time. The others were all late. She fumbled in her bag, feeling her watch strap move around her wrist as she looked for the copy of *A Companion* that she had barely touched at the hospital. She was ready to read it now while waiting for the other women. She was going to return it at the library on the way home.

She couldn't remember exactly where she had left off and flipped through the pages. She spotted a familiar paragraph. She re-read it. The characters were discussing compact powder. A male character said, 'I don't disagree to the trend for compact powder, but I object to their use in public. The way some women use it in public is ungraceful. It makes her charm disappear.' Tarisa looked up and away from the sentence.

She saw Regina coming into the café. Regina apologized for being late, explaining it was due to the difficulty in parking. Tarisa knew it was a challenge for her to fit her Mercedes GLB in smaller parking slots.

They made small talk. The third friend soon arrived, and right away, the conversation became theirs. Tarisa didn't have anything to say about the topic that they launched into—children's activities and classes. The two women didn't seem to notice her lack of interest.

Tarisa began to wriggle her toes just to stay awake. Then, she stretched them as far forward as they could go, moving her feet as if she were dancing ballet and going on pointe. She could feel the leather of her mules bending, edges cracking as the leather broke. The voices of her friends became a backdrop. Their conversation faded away, becoming noise. Another voice became more prominent. She listened to it. It sounded calm and steady, sometimes unsound, but there were patterns, like in water's flow.

There is so much we sign up for that we do not know we do. As if life worked like a website, with Terms and Conditions that we hastily, obliviously, agree to, eyeing the next page. The movement in my story relies on my search to move on from difficulties. In the landscape of the city, where skyscrapers and intersections line life, I am the animal often at a crossroad. Sometimes, when the 'Don't Walk' sign is on, I want to run—as fast as I can, away from a standstill that feels like quicksand. There is no sand in the city—it is a bit farther out, on the East Coast and on Sentosa—and yet, when I stand at a crossroad, I feel I could sink in, disappear. I don't mean that I can disappear (though, on second thought, I suppose I do; I suppose we all do), but that I could use some disappearing. Me. The people around me. We could all disappear for my good at times.

At times, in the isolation of motherhood and sexless monogamy, two things that I have signed up for without reading the Terms and Conditions, my mind takes priority and blankets over reality with adept, nimble hands. It swoops in from above and scoops out a chunk of what was to be before me, leaving a crater where my life should have easily, expectedly, fallen. I miss taking an easily taken step. I don't mean 'miss' as in I nostalgically wish the easily feasible step were near, but as in I err and lose my balance.

My mind threatens me. I am afraid of who I can become, with sadness and despair.

Some call questioning and sliding away from an easily liveable life 'opening a can of worms'. It has not ceased to be interesting to me that ideas can be thought of as squiggly organisms—that are easily crushable. I prefer to think there are no worms; I just tend to be open to asteroids falling into my universe.

Although I am firm about the choice I have made—a mode that I expect can also change—three years existed during which I wished an asteroid would fall upon my body. Those were the years of adjustments. In that period, sometimes, a debris of imagination would fall into my reality. It's powerful what a dot of imagination could do.

I have come to realize that we will into existence the stoppability of our own past to say that a period is over, that the present is different. My present, however, is present in a foggy way. My head is cruising in clouds, drifting through questions only half-answered.

There are subjects that feel like cores out of which concentric thoughts ripple. This movement seems practical. It is optimal, for me to both live and think. 'The unexamined life is not worth living,' Socrates had apparently said, but for me, a thoroughly examined life also makes living barely doable.

My life lived as a bundle of meditations yields a result that is an almost hallucinatory pattern. The ripples of thought quickly move and enlarge. They grow kaleidoscopically before I can capture a thought and hold onto one. I don't want to be holding onto any thought. I want to feel the lightness of being.

(A side question: If I grow quickly while standing in quicksand, will my head escape?)